# Giligadu
## The Lost Days



**CHITRA MUDGAL**

Translated from the Hindi by

**Priyanka Sarkar**

THORNBIRD
NIYOGI BOOKS

Published by
NIYOGI BOOKS
Block D, Building No. 77,
Okhla Industrial Area, Phase-I,
New Delhi-110 020, INDIA
Tel: 91-11-26816301, 26818960
Email: niyogibooks@gmail.com
Website: www.niyogibooksindia.com



Editor: Gita Rajan
Cover illustration and design: Nabanita Das

ISBN: 978-93-89136-05-0
Publication: 2019



Printed at: Niyogi Offset Pvt. Ltd., New Delhi, India

# First Absence

# Crisp Starch

Babu Jaswant Singh could not leave Tommy home even after he had taken him out for his routine morning ablutions.

He left home later than usual today. After all, he is a chronic patient of acidity. These days, he was being visited by constipation though. His stomach would clear only in bits and blobs in spite of drinking a jugful of water every morning. His polyps and fissures had also been bothering him.

He felt a little spasm right when he was set to leave. He had to wait. Jaswant Babu had already added *Kayamchuran* in the *Triphala* powder, for a good measure, just to make things smoother. But things do not seem to be getting smoother. Every night, while taking the medicine, the illusion remained that the morning after would be trouble-free. The morning after would, however, shrug off all responsibility and turn away from him. Now, the prospect of looking at the blood-filled commode would fill him with trepidation. He has increased his dosage of *Himup* without consulting the doctor just to keep the haemoglobin count up. He was well aware that he shouldn't have done so without having consulted the doctor. But he was in a tight spot. His doctor – Doctor Saxena – happened to stay at Kanpur.

Now, he was getting angry at Tommy's antics. Stupid fellow doesn't seem to be able to stand still. He has been sniffing the ground like an ingrate. He was also making strange guttural noises and trying to scare him by posing as if he was running away and was pulling babuji along. But babuji was resolute about not moving anywhere off the bridge. Leaving the bridge would mean getting separated from his usual spot, something he was not willing to do at all.

He realised that Tommy never understood it when the pressure in Babu Jaswant Singh's bladder would build up. However, the uneasiness even after having taken a piss was beyond him. Tommy's antagonistic behaviour was possibly because he was opposing him. Jaswant Babu often found Tommy acting very responsibly when he needed something – now, when he is in a spot, the bastard is acting as if he doesn't need to understand anything, nor can he understand why Jaswant Babu is standing on this particular bridge with him, as if fixed by a nail.

He shouldn't abuse Tommy in spite of being annoyed with him. Babu Jaswant Singh reprimanded himself. Even if he was only thinking up the cusses, he was still cussing. It doesn't take long for one random instance to become a habit. And then, someday, it would roll off his tongue. He had better put a stop to it before that happens.

He had been happy, after his return from Kanpur, that his son and daughter-in-law, by handing over Tommy's responsibilities to him, had thought him capable of something. But now the feeling took root that in this house, he is in reality an elder only to Tommy. Taking care of grandsons Malay and Nilay's whims and fancies did not seem to be part of his fortune.

Tommy isn't any less of a brat. He would wake up as soon as the alarm went off and start whining to wake Jaswant Babu up. As if Jaswant Babu had set the alarm to alert Tommy and not himself. Many a times, Jaswant Babu would keep staring at the alarm, lazily, even if he had woken up. But Tommy couldn't stand the alarm. He'd put his paws out and jump at the stool and drop the clock. This mischief of Tommy's could not be condoned. He complained to his son, Narendra, explaining his misgivings. Tommy shouldn't be tied up in his room. He could jump at him in anger someday. One never knows with an animal. Narendra didn't dispute. Tommy started getting tied up in the passage. Daughter-in-law Sunayana's unhappiness at this mishap was writ large on her face, as if his arrival had exiled Tommy. He had wanted to be brash – her room was the biggest, she could tie him up there, could she not?

He has also noticed that Tommy especially disliked his watching the news. It took him a while to realise that it wasn't the news he disliked but the language. He wouldn't complain if the English news channel was being played. His watching *Aaj Tak* would get the complaints started. He would have barely listened to the headlines that Tommy's whining would have turned into barks filling the living room with terror. Sunayana couldn't bear Tommy's anger. She'd intervene and scold him – 'Please put on some music channel, Babuji! *Aaj Tak* keeps playing all the time anyway.'

Keeping the remote on the armrest of the sofa, Jaswant Babu would very quietly go to the balcony that is his bedroom. The vulgar song '*Mehboob mere, mehboob mere, teri aankhon se zara peene de*' would pierce his ears. Tommy's mannerisms would come to his mind. He'd be sprawled over the floor, bewitched, watching Sushmita Sen's beauty. What he couldn't understand and something nobody could explain to him was – the language which Tommy so despised, how did Sushmita Sen's beauty make it enjoyable?

He used to take Tommy along on his walks even after getting him to relieve himself. But, on the advice of Colonel Swamy he decided against taking him along. The advice was not out of place either. The focus that you need while taking walks cannot be had with Tommy around. On top of that, Tommy's antics could prove fatal for someone his age. Leaving Tommy after his morning ablutions were done would be the wisest course of action. There were younger people at home to indulge his playfulness. Not something he was capable of!

❖

'Oh! Oh! Hope you didn't get hurt too badly? Please wait, don't be in a hurry to get up. Please hold my hand, don't be shy. And don't put too much pressure on your knees. Ok, that's better, hold onto my shoulder. Not like my shoulders are breaking under your weight. Yes, good. Please stand up straight. Yeah, please keep holding onto my hand and try to walk a couple of steps ... everything looks fine.' The stranger held my hand and dusted off the grass and mud stuck to the back of my kurta. Then, lifted the kurta to inspect my legs more carefully. It was evident from the creases and scraping on the pyjamas that the gravel had left scratches on the legs and hips.

This fact seemed to give the stranger a measure of relief: that there were no internal injuries. Otherwise, walking even those few steps would have been impossible with such a fall.

Tommy, leash around his neck, stood at a distance, enjoying the show. The sight of him made Jaswant Babu angry. He wanted to forget all about the stranger beside him and hurl a stone at the rascal's head.

'Oh c'mon! Who wears slippers while taking a walk! Unless you do want to get your bones broken. On top of that you have gotten this loaded gun with you,' complained the stranger, pointing at Tommy.

'....'

'Alright, maybe you have a valid point but you could have just left him at home after his ablutions. Is your house far?' the stranger enquired.

Jaswant Babu pointed towards Glaxo Apartments.

'Ok, Ok, you live in Glaxo? That's quite close. Come, I'll drop you there.' The stranger took his hint.

Jaswant Babu, still a little shaken, could not refuse the offer.

He felt a little thrilled that finding his leash in the stranger's hand, Tommy was behaving like a lamb. That minx!

'Is there a market near your house? If there is, buy a pair of walking shoes in the evening.'

His dilemma was that he did not know much about the markets near his house and he hadn't seen any shoe stores in the local market complex. The stranger asked him his shoe size. Abashed, Jaswant Babu diffidently answered that as far as he could recall, a long time ago his shoe size was seven. He wasn't sure what his size would be now. The stranger laughed aloud. How silly! Jaswant Babu isn't a growing child whose shoe size would keep changing with age. Seven it was then, seven it would be now.

The stranger asked him excitedly whether he went for his walks on the same route every day. He hadn't seen him before – why?

Jaswant Babu clarified. He had taken this route for the first time. Actually, he used to take Tommy for his ablutions and rounds to the big neighbourhood park. Yesterday, the gardener chanced upon them. He reprimanded them – sir, this park is for children – not for dogs to piss and crap in. If reported, he could get fined.

Jaswant Babu felt overwhelmed with gratitude and made to take Tommy's leash from the stranger, near Glaxo. The stranger joked that Jaswant Babu had nothing to fear. He had no intention of partaking of Jaswantji's hospitality. The unevenness of the bridge did not give him the confidence to hand over the leash and walk away. Jaswantji shouldn't worry about him and he won't go anywhere till he has dropped them at the gate. Jaswantji should do one thing though. Did he have children at home? If there were children, there would surely be some *Arnica* at home. If there is, Jaswantji should have 5-6 pills of *Arnica* as soon as he reaches home. Three or four times a day. The internal injury would have settled down by the evening. He should get someone to get it if there weren't any pills handy at home. *Arnica-30.*

Jaswantji wanted to invite the stranger in for a cup of coffee but he didn't have the courage to extend the invitation. At this hour, Sunayana would be getting Malay and Nilay ready for school. The layout of the kitchen had always been out of bounds for him, so he couldn't even get two cups of coffee for the two of them. Though it had been a while since he moved to Delhi from Kanpur, he still felt like a stranger in this house. How could he ask!

'Please don't be so formal.' The stranger seemed to have read his thoughts. 'We will get together some other time. Please excuse me now. Let's meet tomorrow morning. On that same Mayur Vihar flyover; between 6:15-6:30 am. And please leave this darling at home.'

'By the way, my name is Vishnu Narayana Swamy – retired Colonel Swamy. I live in Noida. In Sector 26. I come to your neck of the woods for my walks. The lush greens at the Yamuna banks draw me here. You don't get to smell the sweet fragrance of sugarcane in Noida.'

Jaswant Babu started feeling a little shy.

'I am Jaswant Singh, a retired civil engineer. I live with my son and his family in Glaxo Apartments. I am grateful …'

'Ok, ok, you don't need to do all that. I fully believe that I'll find you absolutely fine on that flyover tomorrow morning. Do take the *Arnica*. I'll take your leave.' He handed over the leash to Jaswant Babu and walked away.

Jaswant Babu kept staring at the Colonel's back climbing up the flyover, till it faded away from his sight.

And right now, on that same flyover, he is waiting for Colonel Swamy.

# Shoes

Tommy could not bear this stillness. He'd start barking at Jaswant Babu out of sheer boredom, or sometimes at the vehicles passing by.

He tried sweet talking, reasoning, since they had waited so long, a little more won't hurt. Tommy should consider his situation too, how he'd be feeling. He was equally restless that Colonel Swamy hadn't reached. His problem was that he could not even get off the flyover; that would mean missing Colonel Swamy. If Colonel Swamy didn't see him he'd think that he had given his walk a miss today. This was not for the irresolute. And definitely not for him.

Jaswant Babu was happy to see that his reasoning worked with Tommy, something he hadn't expected in the least to happen. Tommy stopped barking. The dog holds some respect. The idiot must have thought obeying was better. He was the only one to take him for his walks twice a day, every day, in spite of his constipation. All so that Tommy could smell the greenery, look at the clear skies and the horizon to his fill; yes, he was the only one to give him that opportunity. His anger could prove counter-productive.

Tommy's deepest grouse was that he couldn't go beyond the momentary pleasure of ogling. His rebellious heart urges him to jerk the reins free from the old man's hands and run to his kohl-eyed beloved! Why doesn't the old man look at himself? Acts like Raja Harishchandra but the old man is no less of a pervert. He has often divined that. The dump-yard next to United Apartments is no place for him to pee but that stubborn old man would not let him walk past it. This happens in the evenings when the jeans-clad young vivacious girls would be stepping out of United to go to the ice cream vendor in front of the gate of Samachar. He was forced to relieve himself there. He knew that the old man wouldn't move from that spot until the girls walked past them, licking their ice-creams. The old man has progressed from merely scolding and has resorted to hitting him with his stick to control him. Never took him anywhere without the stick.

❖

Jaswant Babu gets up suddenly with his eyes towards the right. His disappointed expression starts changing. Hazy distant figures seem to be jogging from Noida towards them. Judging from the fitness of the figure at the start of the line, he felt it had to be Colonel Swamy. Leaving the others behind. He couldn't understand why he couldn't see the figures more clearly. Was his eyesight fading? The next moment Jaswant Babu laughed at his own impatience. He needs patience not better vision. Colonel Swamy is coming. However, the hazy figures started getting clearer and left him disappointed. Colonel Swamy used to wear white shorts even towards the end of November. The figure in the front was wearing a jogging suit. That too a black one, something the colonel would never wear. In fact, he had brought back to life the viruses of Jaswant Babu's own likes and dislikes.

Sunayana had been noticing the changes in his behaviour.

Earlier, he didn't have a fixed time for his walks. He would go out as soon as he'd wake up. Nowadays, he'd diligently set an alarm every night. He had also been turning increasingly antagonistic towards Tommy. He would return him almost as soon he'd take him out. Sunayana had been noticing the house-bound Tommy getting depressed day by day. As soon as he saw anyone getting out of the house, his tail would start wagging while he looked at them greedily, his heart aflutter. Sunayana never said anything initially thinking that maybe he had to relieve himself urgently. But when she saw no change in his behaviour, she was forced to reprimand him.

Jaswant Babu had been waiting for this very moment. In fact, what amazed him was that he hadn't been called to the docks earlier.

He looked at the expressions on Sunayana's face, ignored them and retorted. Probably for the first time ever.

Taking Tommy on long walks was not possible for him. He couldn't handle both of them – Tommy and himself – at the same time. He can't be running marathons given his age!

He didn't want to get his bones broken and become dependent, at the mercy of others.

Sunayana was surprised. Such a harsh response to a mundane query! She couldn't understand why he got so annoyed at her legitimate question.

❖

'Good morning, Sir! Nobody would believe that you had a fall just yesterday.'

He had probably laughed for the first time in Delhi.

'Sir, the fall was just an excuse to meet you.'

'Hahahahaha!' Colonel Swami roared out a laugh. Jaswant Babu joined him, giving a perfect accompaniment to the round of laughter.

When the bout of merriment ended, the colonel said, 'Should we start walking now?'

His gaze suddenly went to Jaswant Babu's feet.

'Can a walk start without shoes? Lean against the railing and take off your slippers.' He took out a box of Phoenix shoes from the rucksack on his back. 'Wear these. I had almost forgotten.'

'Actually…'

'I knew you wouldn't have been able to find a shoe store, so I got them. That's all. I also knew you wouldn't have been able to find *Arnica*.'

Colonel Swamy took out a slim bottle from the pocket of his shorts and told Jaswant Babu, 'Open your mouth.'

After putting four to five pills in Jaswant Babu's mouth, he put the bottle in Jaswant Babu's kurta pocket and ordered him to take the pills every four hours without fail.

Jaswant Babu felt emotional while taking out the shoes from the shoe box and tying the shoelaces.

'Fit?' Colonel Swamy chuckled like a child as soon as Jaswant Babu stood up after tying the shoelaces.

His shyness also vanished. 'They fit so well, almost as if I picked them up from the shoe store myself.'

'That's how I too felt, as if you had gone with me to the store.'

Colonel Swamy also resolved Jaswant Babu's dilemma about his bathroom slippers.

'Let's pack them in the same shoe box and put it behind the bushes.'

Jaswant Babu nodded his head in agreement.

'Shall we go?'

'Let us.' Feeling the warmth of the soles of the new shoes, Jaswant Babu started competing with Colonel Swamy.

He didn't discuss the price because he had thought he'd find it on the shoe box. He'll put the money in an envelope tomorrow morning before the walk. Narendra must have also been noticing the condition of his bathroom slippers. Must also know how dangerous it is to go walking in them with a nuisance such as Tommy. Didn't it ever occur to him to buy walking shoes?

His eyes welled up.

❖

In his youth, Jaswant Babu was very particular about his attire. Especially his shoes. Narendra's mother used to find his tastes a waste of money. Strict accounting in the name of disciplining the children! Even if an inch of pencil was left, they wouldn't get a new one. Worn out soles of school shoes would get covered by scraps of tyre tubes. Going for school picnics was not allowed. Why spend money and then keep wondering about the kids the whole day? If books got lost, they were told to borrow them and study. Without sternness, they would not understand the value of money. We want this, we want that – that won't work. They have their life in front of them to fulfil all their desires. They can buy whatever they want with their own money. He was disciplined at the right time, which is why he turned out fine. It is no joke to have been born in the house of the talukdar of thirty-two villages.

Narendra's mother would invariably get annoyed whenever he brought up the past. She had no interest in hearing about his exploitative talukdars. All she cared about was her children! They had not dropped down from the skies! And it wasn't like she was asking for fancy rides or frivolous luxuries for them. The children were not blind. Nor were they dumb ignoramuses for his varied collection of footwear to go unnoticed by them. Trying to discipline the children without setting an example first was like trying to light an oil lamp without oil or wick. Will the lamp throw any light?

He tried to impress upon Narendra's mother scores of times that the status of a man was not judged by his house or car but his shoes. If the shoes are not stiff and sturdy the man's gait gets ruined. Her stubborn mind refused to accept these subtle social nuances and he had to just make his peace with it.

A few months ago when he had set out for Delhi from Kanpur and Narendra had asked him to clear out the unwanted things in the house, he had been astonished to find a lot of his shoes, each polished and put in different polythene bags by Narendra's mother in a wooden chest.

Narendra had been shocked.

His dismay wasn't because of Babuji's love for shoes, he had known about the shoes. The variety had boggled him for a minute. But that fascination had also not stayed too long. What had surprised him was the care Mother had taken of them. They looked like they had just been bought from the showroom.

Practicality won the day. Narendra bluntly told him not to be sentimental. Lugging the shoes all the way to Delhi was out of question. There was no place there to store them, neither had anybody the time to look after them. Their shoe sizes were different, so it wasn't as if he could wear them. Leaving them here for so long was not advisable. Leather does not take long to mottle. Would be better if someone from the village could pick them up. Babuji could keep a couple that he liked. In any case he needed a pair for the winters. Shoe prices have sky rocketed.

Narendra's apathy had angered Jaswant Babu.

He refused to take a single pair along. Whether they be cheap or expensive. It has been a year since the bones in his feet had started growing. He had gotten a few injections. He could not bear the rub of leather. He had spent the last winter in toed-socks and chappals. He'd do that in Delhi too.

Narendra, indifferent and indignant, had retorted, 'As you please.'

❖

'Look at that! Hello, what thoughts are you lost in Mr Singh?

'Can you see the mud and bamboo hut in the middle of the fields! For the guard! Looks so beautiful. Just like it used to be back home in Kerala.

'Oh my god! Look at those mynahs – drinking water from the drains with their beaks, just like people stand in a queue for food at weddings.

'Do you know what *gili* means?'

He wondered whether Colonel Swamy was talking about '*gilli-danda*.' But he shook his head to show ignorance.

'Gili means bird. *Giligadu* means birds. Actually, in Malayalam we call it – *kilikalu*. I have turned it into *giligadu* in Hindi.

'You are not even aware that we have beautiful birds at home.'

'Do you like birds?'

'That I do.' Colonel Swamy started smirking. 'But my Giligadu are my twin granddaughters. Always jumping, dancing, screaming, laughing … Kumudini and Katyayini … always up to something.'

Jaswant Babu's eyes sparkled like stars, amazed, glittering. 'Twins? How old?'

'Going to turn four. Studying in Nursery. With schoolbags on their backs. With colourful tiffin boxes and water bottles.'

'They don't just share the leftovers in their boxes, Mr Singh, they jump around and share all the songs they've learnt in school with expressions, my Giligadus.'

*Hathi Raja bahut bade,*
*Soond uthakar kahaan chale?*
*Mere ghar mein aao na,*
*Halwa puri khao na!*
(Elephant king, huge and grand,
Where're you off to, trunk upturned?
Come, please come to our place,
Come have *halwa puri* please!)

'Do you know what happens before they sing?

'They hand over a pencil and paper and make me

sit on a chair and pretend to be a judge. Ceremoniously order – Appu! We are going to dance and sing really well. You just need to rate us like Ma'am.

'I give them both zero.

'And don't even ask about the cat and mouse game that follows. I look for hideouts in every possible corner of the house to escape their clutches but they always manage to find me. And then the punishment that follows, horrifying.

'Appu, stand on the bench with your hands pulling your ears.'

'You?' Jaswant Babu asked horrified.

'Who else?'

'Then?'

'Then what? You have to suffer the punishment. Have to stand on the dining table, till my Giligadu are satisfied.'

'Spoilt rotten.' Jaswant Babu laughed.

Colonel Swamy joined him and said that he has never suffered such a court martial in his entire career.

He narrated another of Giligadu's escapades as soon as their laughter subsided. It was just a few days ago, his middle daughter-in-law, Anushree – Giligadu's mother – complained that the darlings have not been brushing their teeth at night. Their mouth smelled and they had bacteria in their teeth on top of that! She had patiently explained for a long time to both of them the importance of brushing their teeth at night. But they paid no attention; the only person to get Giligadu to behave is Appu. He told them both sternly that if they didn't brush their teeth at night, they won't get their morning kiss from Appu.

He had to scold them. They got after him. They agreed to brush their teeth only if Appu brushed his teeth too, with them. They have never seen Appu brush his teeth. Won't Appu's teeth go bad?

He was left with no choice but to brush with them every night although Kumudini and Katyayini slept before him. Also, their bed time was his drinking time. At that time, he used to sip on his favourite whiskey, *Royal Challenge*. But now, he has to brush before drinking.

The entire household has been teasing him that Appu was putty in Giligadu's hands.

Seeing that Jaswant Babu's curiosity was aroused, Colonel Swamy told him about the rest of his family members. His wife had died many years ago. He has three sons and three daughters-in-law. The eldest son has two adolescent sons, Shreedharan and Shreenivasan. The middle son and daughter-in-law's children are Giligadu. The youngest son and daughter-in-law are Shyamali and Prabhakaran who do not have any children and they are in no hurry either as they are focusing on their careers. The whole family lives together. Even though they have flats of their own, the children don't want to leave him alone. They have been especially attentive since their mother's death. They have decided to live together even after his death as they feel that they will grow stronger if they live together. They have put their flats on rent. They are repaying the loans through the rent. Since he had been posted in far-off regions and non-family stations, Appu had been able to enjoy family life only in bits. The children understand that pain of his and ensure that he receives all joys of a family life.

'Are you looking at the sugarcanes swaying, Mr Singh? The wind makes the standing crop dance to its beats.'

They turned around on the Pontoon bridge and parted ways at Glaxo flyover.

Jaswant Babu felt like proposing to Colonel Swamy that they meet on the Glaxo bridge the next morning.

He was a little disappointed that Colonel Swamy had anticipated what he was going to ask for.

'Even early morning, the Mayur Vihar crossing is fairly busy. The empty police station just stands tall and grand. The place is safe. Meeting there will be best. It is not safe to wait in front of Glaxo. I don't fear for myself, I have faced danger all my life. I am used to it, but you are not.

'The 1965 war had gone on for twenty-two days. 1971 for thirteen. But … the soldier doesn't only fight in wars. He has to fight when preparing for the war … that is the real battle,' Colonel Swamy had muttered.

# Ramvati Somvati

Babu Jaswant had started feeling that the air was getting chillier with the cold manifesting in shivers and stuffy noses. Sneezing alone could relieve him from the stuffiness. But he didn't want to sneeze right now. His late wife had associated sneezing with ill omen. Some really strange thoughts crossed his mind just a while ago. The killer Blue-line buses had started competing with jet planes and considered pedestrians frequenting the road as mere worms and insects who had no right to be there. The roads were not for these worms. The buses alone had the sole right to the roads and footpaths. How could they spare the ones who dared to take away their rights? And why should they? This was their way of teaching pedestrians a lesson.

Have they opened their killer jaws somewhere nearby?

He felt ashamed. Couldn't he think of good things early in the morning? Did he have to revel in bad thoughts? Had there been a mishap wouldn't it have shown on the faces of those coming from Noida and Nagarjuna Apartments?

Maybe after having waited a while for him, Colonel Swamy would have taken off towards Pontoon bridge to complete his daily quota. It's not like he lived close. By his estimation, which could be incorrect, the colonel's house was some four to five kilometres away. He knows this because on enquiring whether the colonel didn't get tired just walking from his home to their meeting spot, Colonel Swamy had belly-laughed as if he had said something silly and childish. That Jaswant Babu was forgetting that he had worked in the Army, where officers of all ranks had to kccp themselves fit by running at the crack of dawn.

Had he gone towards Pontoon bridge, Colonel Swamy would have surely turned around and reached this flyover. It doesn't take longer than half an hour to walk there.

And that is after taking into account the time he would take to admire the lushness of the crops.

❖

'Do something …' Colonel Swamy had laughed and turned towards Jaswant Babu during the walk on their fourth meeting. 'Kurta-Pajama is not appropriate attire for walking. Loose clothes slacken your pace. Buy two pairs of "Lux Cottswool". It is only going to get colder.

'You can wear a coat or a jacket if you still feel cold.

'Let me know if you won't be able to buy, I'll buy it for you from Atta market.'

An embarrassed Jaswant Babu immediately remonstrated. He hadn't accepted money for the shoes and now Jaswantji didn't want to owe him for yet another thing. That day, the wound had scared him and he was also unaware of Acharya Niketan Market nearby. He will not be slack this time. He will go to the market and buy pairs of his choice. In fact, tomorrow he will be seen by Colonel Swamy only in Lux Cottswool.

He did feel good that there was someone who cared about not just warmth but also about cut and fit and appearance. In the shape he had always wanted to be in. He didn't realise when the fire had gotten doused. Whether the fire had been cooled or he chose to stop living, to just drift along with whatever life threw his way and simply exist.

He was suddenly nostalgic about Kanpur, his hometown. As if a lamp had been lit somewhere.

People might consider Kanpur a backward, dirty, wayward and riot-prone city but for him it was synonymous with happiness and comfort. Not for nothing was it referred to as the country's Manchester.

You had to just ask someone to get whatever you want and it would be at your doorstep within the hour. Whatever you want. You can pay on delivery or if you are broke, pay when you are solvent. The shopkeeper would never dare to ask you for payment. Now, all shops have telephones. Just a matter of minutes.

While in service he had lived in a number of big cities during his transfers but had always managed to wangle a transfer back to Kanpur. He had bought a 500 *gaz* plot in Jawaharnagar sometime ago and kept building a house on it as per plan. Luckily, the municipal corporation built a beautiful garden right in front of it. There is a banyan tree smack in the middle of the garden, which the Muncipal Corporation has left untouched. A lot of birds congregate there. Dawn and dusk are made joyous and lively by their chirrups, filling one's being with peace.

He had given the room in the backyard garage to Ramasre Pasi, whose wife, Sunguniya, would do all the household chores, be it sweeping the main house or sprinkling water at the height of summers.

Narendra's mother couldn't bear his bratty, boisterous children though.

Jaswant Babu would try to placate her. Let them do whatever they want to in the backyard. Consider your benefits. The children's noises liven up the house. Otherwise, there is no dearth of robbers.

Unfortunately, Ramasre Pasi passed away before Narendra's mother. He had gone to his village on being summoned by his older brother. They got the news a fortnight after that Ramasre was one of the twenty-one who had died of alcohol poisoning in Birhun village.

They couldn't believe it. They had never seen him drunk. Sunguniya revealed that every time he got drunk, he slipped into bed soundlessly. He feared them and hence, never made a sound.

The wailing Sunguniya with her three children was taken back to their village by her elder brother-in-law. Her wails stayed with them like a feverish nightmare.

Narendra's mother felt relieved in spite of feeling bad for Sunguniya and got Ramrati Baarin to take over post-haste.

She got Sunguniya's things packed up in bundles and got the garage cleaned and sprinkled it with holy water.

The gates were jangled almost a fortnight later.

Sunguniya was at the gates, standing there with her mud-soaked children.

She fell down at Narendra's mother's feet crying. Her children also started crying.

The tyrannous mother melted at this sight. She asked Sunguniya how she was. She should have sent a relative to pick up her things instead of coming. If she had come to stay, then living alone in this immoral, unsafe city was a bad idea.

Sunguniya's cries stopped and she said in a quavering voice, 'I came here on the strength of my faith in my goddess-like mistress. Her shelter will embolden me.'

She was open and honest when it came to discussing her pay. She will do her mistress's bidding as before. Nobody can dare to take over her work! No, she won't let the other maid walk in. She'll take up work in other houses nearby in whatever time she can spare from working here. She just wants to raise her children. She will get her son to work at a dhaba or hotel once he turns twelve. They'll manage!

She didn't want to go back to the village at any cost. Mistress should not try to persuade. Back in the village, the older brother-in-law was very exploitative. He was trying to get her married off to an older friend so that he could take over their share of the property. So, she ran off to the bus stop on the pretext of morning ablutions and rushed straight to her mistress in Kanpur. She is safe now. If her brother-in-law came here to take her away, she'll go to the police station with mistress and tell them that she didn't want to go back with that wolf.

Her familiarity annoyed Narendra's mother in spite of the feeling of pity. How dare a chit of a girl land at her doorstep after kicking away her relatives. She must have been carrying on with her husband, that's how things were with these low-caste people, their morals always flexible.

Jaswant Babu scolded Narendra's mother so much that she drowned the night in a pool of tears. He might be a weak man but how dare she imagine him having an affair with just about anyone and everyone? He had been very discreet in his earlier affairs and not a whiff of it got around. There was no way of her getting to know about them. There was no point castigating him for sins he had not committed.

What annoyed Jaswant Babu was the fact that though a consummate homemaker, Narendra's mother never cultivated any outside interests or hobbies that would rivet his interest. He acknowledges her adeptness at managing the house and always will. She was quick on her feet like a genie, things materialised as soon as you asked for them. Would he have cheated on her if she had an equally quick wit? Not something that should be said but he has seen fresh, clean-as-slate women become so interesting that any man would wish that their wife was such.

Narendra had also questioned Sunguniya's presence like his mother. So, he also brought Jaswant Babu to the docks and insisted she leave the garage so that there was no drama in future. He had heard that Sunguniya has taken up a full time job at BSP leader, Ram Khilawan Yadav's home in the next lane. His house was big enough to accommodate Sunguniya. Why can't she shift there?

Jaswant Babu had countered saying that she had not taken up that job since Jaswant Babu was moving out of Kanpur. She had taken up that job much earlier, when Narendra's mother was still alive. It doesn't matter where she works since nobody lives in the house. Her presence keeps the house safe.

He can never forget that on the day of Narendra's departure, Sunguniya had confronted him, teary-eyed. Master was leaving for Delhi with his son and daughter-in-law. May he be happy there but he should maintain his house here. Sunguniya should also get the opportunity to care for him.

He had given Sunguniya the telephone number and address of the house in Delhi on a piece of paper.

She had gotten Ram Khilawan Yadav's eldest daughter to dial the number. Sunayana couldn't swallow her own spit when she heard Sunguniya's voice on the other side of the line.

Sunguniya had assured him that the house was safe and fine but she didn't know about the condition indoors. It would have been different had she been given the house keys. How was he? She was thinking of getting Ramvati and Somvati admitted into a government school with Ram Khilawan's help. What does Master think?

He remembers telling Sunguniya that nobody could do what Ram Khilawan could. He was very influential in the area. She shouldn't think twice before getting his help to get Ramvati and Somvati admitted. Education is very important. He only had one advice if Sunguniya was fine with it. Since they hadn't been admitted yet, she should get their names changed. She should name them Kumudini and Katyayini. Sunguniya could not understand the names. She handed over the phone to Ram Khilawan's daughter asking him to tell her the names since she will be going with them for the school admissions. Ram Khilawan's daughter was happy to hear the names. He had another piece of advice. The surname should not be Pasi but Aasre (shelter). Katyayini Aasre, Kumudini Aasre.

Sunguniya then asked him what she should call her youngest.

Jaswant Babu had not yet been able to find a name for him.

❖

'Do you know where I had hidden your shoe box? On top of the Godrej almirah in my room. Had Giligadu gotten their hands on them again, the shoes would have been in tatters by the time they reached you.

'And the bribe I had to pay to get the shoes from them, oh god!'

What had happened was that when Colonel Swamy was returning home in the evening, shoe box in hand, Giligadu, dressed for their play date, spotted him. They assumed that Appu had gotten them a gift like always. They snatched the box away even before he could explain himself and each wore a shoe on one foot. And on top of that, the brats, wearing one large-sized shoe each, started running around inside the house. Colonel Swamy ran after them beseechingly, scared lest they take a tumble and break their heads or noses.

Shyamali saved him.

She scolded Giligadu and ordered them to take the shoes off or she will lock them in the bathroom with lizards where the lizards might even bite them.

Shyamali's threat worked. Not only did they take off the shoes but also helped Shyamali put them back in the box.

But they didn't shy away from blackmailing their Appu. They ordered him to get them shoes the next day.

Appu will take them to the market to choose. He will also take them to McDonald's after shopping. Chicken Burger with French Fries. They will get a toy with the burger. They had seen it on the TV. From there, they will go to Nirula's for ice-cream.

Colonel Swamy was grateful that he could get away without much damage.

'I really enjoyed with the squirrels though. Have you also gone to McDonald's with your grandsons?

'Haven't? Then you should take them sometime. It will be fun. You'll feel as if you are the same age as them. Nowadays, it is common to celebrate birthdays there.' Colonel Swamy told him in an amused tone.

He also told him that he had tried to start this practice at home but his daughters-in-law opposed it. Such strict bores! Started muttering that this is not done. The children's birthdays will be celebrated the way they have been till now. The way their mother-in-law had. The way all festivals were celebrated. Even if the children pleaded a million times. How else would they know how their grandmother used to celebrate their birthdays?

That reminded Jaswant Babu that Malay's birthday was next week: on the 18th of November. He'll discuss with Malay about celebrating his birthday at McDonald's. He will foot the bill. However much it be. Malay was delighted to hear his proposal. He told him that he had already planned to celebrate his birthday at McDonald's. He had discussed it with his parents as well. They had also agreed. But he had planned it with his friends. His family was not included in the plan. Mother always found birthday celebrations at home a hassle. Last year, his friends' antics had tired her. She had told him then to take his friends out. Now, he is old enough.

Malay explained the programme to him.

There would be fourteen people counting his friends from Glaxo, Kirti and Nirman. Father has booked a table at McDonald's for fourteen. Three cars from the society will go, one of Saguna's, the other of Vivek's and the third ours. Father will get a driver from the office for our car that day.

No, Dadu, I won't take any grownup with me. The party will become very boring and the drivers will be there anyway.'

Jaswant Babu said, a little let down, 'Ok, don't take me to McDonald's but what do you want from your grandfather for your birthday?'

'Hmmmm … Get me Adnan Sami's CD.'

'Where do I get that from?'

'From any CD store.'

'Something nearby?'

'Nope.'

'Then?'

'You'll have to go to Palika Bazaar.'

'Will the two of you go with me?'

'No.'

'Why?'

'Have to study.'

Jaswant Babu was disheartened. It wasn't the children's fault. He was being taught to stay within his limits. He was being made to understand that they didn't need anyone. It was for this reason that he didn't gift Malay-Nilay any blocks sets, mechanics or puzzles. He used to find it strange that Narendra and his wife would get the children toys without them even asking for them. These toys would keep the children busy for a long time. They never felt the need for anyone. They would come to Kanpur with these toys. They weren't even interested in playing with the neighbourhood kids and they weren't interested in including these excited kids in their games. Wouldn't even let them touch their toys. The kids were being taught to be loners in the name of developing their intelligence, that too to such an extent that they could neither connect with their families nor be able to create familial bonds of their own.

# Gathri Mein Laaga Chor*
## (Beware! Thief!)

Jaswant Babu looked at the rising sun lighting up a hazy sky, taking a break from his slowly ebbing dismay.

How did these ants climb on to my legs? Maybe they were tired of staying on the bridge.

School buses had started plying. Which meant that he hadn't realised that Time wasn't waiting for Colonel Swamy, only he was. Which was why he was still waiting on the bridge. But till when should he wait? Rickshaws had started dropping bus passengers at the bus stop from the pockets in the colony and were waiting near the bridge, for the passengers from Noida from across the road.

Tommy, his eyes closed but scrutinising him, was pretending to sleep. 'Let's go, Tommy!' Jaswant Babu said a little belligerently.

---

* A mystic verse on the ephemeral nature of worldly possessions, composed by the Poet-Saint Kabir, made popular in bhajan form by K.C. Dey and as a popular film song by Manna Dey.

Tommy protested by neither opening his eyes nor wagging his tail. Not even when Jaswant Babu yanked at his collar with the leash.

Maybe Colonel Swamy had to go somewhere all of a sudden. Lot of responsibilities in a joint family and the patriarch has to take care of them. That's what he did in Kanpur. Narendra never attended any birthdays, weddings or funerals.

Kanpur beckoned him again.

He never wanted to come to Delhi nor was there a single day that he liked here.

Earlier, he had sauntered in as a guest, spent a few days, left Narendra's mother and gone back to Kanpur.

She stayed with her son, daughter-in-law and grandsons for however long she wanted and then she would get Narendra to call him. That she was worried for him. The last time, she had worried that his asthma was acting up. He seemed short of breath. Maybe his BP was also high. He is very careless with his medication. Narendra should send her in Shatabdi. Ramasre will pick her up.

She would keep singing praises of her son and daughter-in-law for months.

She had left saunth and mawa-filled gond laddoos in a canister for the winters. She had made them in Kanpur and filling the canister had given Sunguniya blisters on her hands. The laddoos got over within a week. Narendra put in a repeat request. All Narendra has for breakfast is a laddoo with a glass of milk. Not only do Malay and Nilay savour them but feed them to their friends in the society as well. Thankfully, Sunayana caught them in the act and gave them a good yelling. 'Amma laboured over the laddoos and you are giving them away to all and sundry!'

Narendra got her to make UP-style dahi-badas a few times. In fact, he got her to cook for a party at home for his colleagues. His boss's wife insisted on getting the recipe for *rasajes* after eating them.

While getting off the uneven Glaxo flyover, ruing over Colonel Swamy's absence, the chill in his bones and the dryness of his lips, Jaswant Babu rapped his knuckles mentally: if only he could dish out culinary delights like Narendra's mother, maybe his daughter-in-law Sunayana would have found him to be of some use around the house. What use was an old imbecile who could only eat and shit!

❖

'Do you like idlis, Mr Singh?' Colonel Swamy had asked Jaswant Babu.

When he replied with a 'sometimes', Colonel Swamy sang praises of his eldest daughter-in-law, Madhavi, who made melt-in-your-mouth idlis. She knew that three of his teeth in the upper jaw and two in the lower one were loose and he could not bite hard things. He had to forego a lot of his favourite foods. Madhavi made it her mission to make him delicious food that he didn't have to chew too hard. She was making idlis with sambar and coconut chutney for dinner. Idlis are available everywhere but the ones Madhavi makes are the tastiest.

He will get Madhavi to pack a few idlis for Jaswant Babu when he leaves for his morning walk. She will pack them in banana leaves so that they stay warm till the time he eats them. Does Jaswant Babu like his chutney bland or spicy? He remembered that Jaswant Babu suffers from piles and could not eat spicy food. He will get the chutney made less spicy.

'Have you done any sight-seeing in Delhi?

'Haven't yet?

'No excuses.

'Look at Delhi with me through my eyes, Mr Singh. I challenge you that you will fall in love with the city and wonder why you have been estranged from it for so long.'

That was a lovely day with balmy weather. Five hundred rupees for eight hours in a DLY taxi, Colonel Swamy took him to visit Delhi's historical sites. And they were sitting in the ruins next to Qutub Minar sipping home-made rasam from Colonel Swamy's thermos.

Jaswant Babu was having such delicious rasam after a long time. Whenever his daughter, Shalini, came to visit them from Trivandrum, he would always request her to make rasam.

It was when Jaswant Babu praised the rasam, that Colonel Swamy had wanted to know his opinion on idlis.

Jaswant Babu got a little emotional while talking about his likes. Actually, since his move to Delhi, he had forgotten that he had any favourite foods. He had to often eat things he couldn't chew or his body found difficult to digest. There was no fixed time for when he would get his breakfast, leave alone him getting to eat things he liked.

He would leaf through *Hindustan Times* after his morning walk, waiting for the call for his breakfast and lemon tea only to be told by Sunayana that she will cook his *daliya* as soon as the kids left for school. The sound of the door closing would give him the solace that the children had left for school and he would now get his breakfast.

After a few minutes he would be handed an over-brewed cup of lemon-less tea and be told that he would have to drink his tea without lemon today. Sunayana was under the impression that there were lemons in the fridge. When she looked for them, she realised that maybe Narendra had used them for the dinner salad as well as his morning cuppa.

After a few minutes, she would peek into his room to inform him that daliya had gotten over and would not be coming till evening. Would he like to have chilla for breakfast? He would remember that day before yesterday, they had had mungers made for Sunayana's cousin, Kusum, who had come from Pitampura with family and there would be some leftover dal paste. Sunayana might not have been able to come up with a way to use them till now. She had probably checked with others on ways to use it up. The others might have turned down the chillas. He was in no position to turn them down. Family can express likes and dislikes, not those who come to live with them.

There was a time when it had mattered what he liked – he prefers Indian food. Neither did he like nor could he digest all that pizza, burger, noodles, Russian salad, etc., etc. He had thought of letting Narendra know about his aversion to these things in the first week of his arrival in Delhi. He couldn't eat just about anything and everything. His mother never fed him leftovers and his stomach wasn't used to it. He liked his rotis straight off the gas. The ones in the casserole always got a little hard to chew. Narendra lectured him in turn and told him that in this house, he should keep his likes and dislikes to himself. His reply was valid too, he should move ahead with the times.

Amma had always cared for his likes. Shalini and he had to eat whatever their father wanted to eat. On top of that, he had ruled that neither child could put back anything from their plates nor leave anything in it and disrespect food.

Although IIT was in Kanpur, Jaswant Babu had ordered Narendra not to stay at home but in the hostel. He will focus on his education better. He was not allowed to complain about the terrible mess food. He wasn't the only one eating it. Everybody ate the same food. One has to make a few sacrifices to become successful in life. Jaswant Babu had said all that.

Whenever Amma wanted to drop off some home-cooked food, Jaswant Babu would get rough.

Once, Amma was getting homemade shakkarparas and jackfruit pickle sent on the sly with Ramsevak Kaka who was visiting from the village. When he found out, he threw away the boxes of food hanging from Kaka's cycle.

Jaswant Babu was shocked to hear this litany.

He realised the futility of discussing the importance of discipline or letting bygones be bygones with Narendra. He had considered all of that when he had been so strict with the children. It is understandable that Narendra won't be able to fathom his reasons. How else was NTPC Chief Engineer, Mr Narendra Kushwaha, going to air his bitterness but by expressing his displeasure?

What Narendra doesn't remember is that he had liquidated his fixed deposits to pay for his Electrical Engineering course. Without thinking twice! It is true that he had to work hard to keep him in the hostel. Unlike his colleagues, he wasn't corrupt and had to work twice as hard.

Nothing to be proud of but he couldn't forget this incident for the longest time even after coming back from that week in Bombay. In spite of his friends pressuring him to, he couldn't take out the money to pay the hefty fee for this beautiful but unsuccessful film actress to sleep with him.

His colleague Vivek Awasthi had teased him.

'What kind of a Thakur are you? Are you in fact one? I have my doubts.'

❖

Tommy tried to drag him towards the Pomeranian bitch walking on their side. He would have dragged him had he been even a little careless. It was then that he remembered that he didn't have the stick. How could he have been so careless? Tommy had made him fall once already! Would havc today as well. Such a nuisance. He wanted to let go of his leash, let him run away.

But he could not let go.

# Second Absence

# Stench

This morning! Jaswant Babu tossed and turned on his bed and waited till the first light of the morning to go out to the narrow road of the flyover in Mayur Vihar.

Last afternoon, it had struck Jaswant Babu that Colonel Swamy had given him his telephone number on a piece of paper a few weeks ago. He had tossed it under his pillow with his other papers. Thinking that he would be meeting him the next day. That he would never really need that piece of paper.

He had a tough time finding that piece of paper.

He also felt a little exasperated with himself for having kept useless documents such as old prescriptions, X-ray reports, prescriptions by his Kanpur doctor, Doctor Saxena, that he would never need, alongside his other important documents.

At least, he got to sort his documents on this pretext.

He felt like he had discovered a pot of gold as soon as he found the piece of paper.

With the pot of gold, he also found the hand-made birthday card sent to him by his grandchildren from

Trivandrum. Jaswant Babu was overcome with a wave of emotion and memories.

The card reminded him that his birthday had just come and gone without a sound or a creak.

Narendra had not deemed it fit to mention his birthday.

Earlier, on his birthday, when Narendra would be the first to call him specially and pay his respects, he would be touched and would shower blessings on him. Narendra used to be the first one to call every year. It always annoyed Shalu. She'd called very early in the morning to wish only because she wanted to beat her brother to it and be the first to wish.

In retrospect, Narendra was probably right. What is the point of remembering the date that only increased his helplessness!

Maybe Narendra had not reminded him for this very reason.

He took hold of Colonel Swamy's number and called him some ten times. Then felt the weight of Sunayana's disapproving glance. Which he had not actually seen, only felt.

Who have you been trying to call for the last half an hour, Babuji? You have been blocking other important calls. Narendra charges his phone in the morning. If the phone is ringing it could be just two things. The phone could be in need of repair or there was no one home. Whether the phone is working or not can be found out by calling 197. They can even be asked to call the number. You'd know for sure what the reason is.

Jaswant Babu thought it best to leave the phone behind.

He was still hopeful. He will meet Colonel Swamy the next morning. He hadn't been able to meet him on just one day. He should not think that he won't be meeting him the next morning. Whatever may have happened! He should find peace in the fact that Colonel Swamy was not one to keep unhappiness or grief to himself. He was open, an extrovert.

Else he would've truly been lonely in Delhi and missed Kanpur even more.

'You will not be able to get over the death of your wife if you stay here. You'll forget all your unhappiness in Delhi. Grandchildren are the best antidote for grief, you'll be so busy with them,' Mr Ahluwalia from Gumti had explained.

Mr Ahluwalia doesn't have a computer at home. If he had, his words would have been different.

He had insisted that Jaswant Babu should correspond with him regularly. Jaswantji had thought of penning a letter. The first obstacle was: what to write? That he couldn't find a second childhood with his grandchildren? That he thought of finding it with Narendra but he had himself been too busy then. Now he had the time. But, Narendra was to busy to give him any time. And why was that? Lately, it seems, Jaswant Babu has been sacrificed at the altar of Narendra's computer. He couldn't give what the computer could. His experiences were not worth narrating. His knowledge limited. How does he connect with his childhood?

'Dadu, tell us something. A quiz question needs to be answered quickly.'

'Ask.'

'Of the Pyramids of Egypt, of the Seven Wonders, which is the largest and whose?'

'All I remember is that it is of a fourth generation royal.'

'Just this much won't do.' Malay was disappointed.

'Ok, how big is it?'

'I don't remember that either. Have forgotten.'

'Ok, I'll look it up online.'

Malay came back a bit later and told him. The biggest pyramid is of the king of Egypt, Khufu and his wife, Mekbara and it is 481 feet over ground level. He was sad that he didn't know the answer and had lost the quiz. He had to answer the Zee TV quizmaster over the phone.

❖

'Knock, Knock.' Jaswant Babu was knocking on the door with his heart beating fast. It didn't open. Maybe it was latched. How does he enter? Somebody whispered in his ear, Who? Who is it? Answer? Why isn't the bolt opening?

Uneasiness never becomes apparent. It only whispers,

'Listen? Push the doors, push harder. The door must be unlatched. It always is.'

❖

It was probably a Sunday. Not probably, it was definitely Sunday. Colonel Swamy had taken him to Kalindi Kunj which is adjacent to the Yamuna barrage of Noida. The greenery really pleased him. Such a huge garden and not too far from his house at that. He had no idea. Narendra had never mentioned it either. He would have enjoyed hearing about it even if he couldn't go. How had Colonel Swamy asked him? Have you been to Mathura and Vrindavan? Don't worry if you haven't. We'll make a plan and go. Not as if they are too far. You have to cross Ballabhgarh and Faridabad and you will be in Mathura. For now, let us go to Kalindi Kunj. It will be the same as being in Vrindavan. It has the Yamuna and a garden. All it doesn't have is Krishna. And then started laughing and said that they were being foolish to think that, in spite of the presence of two Krishnas.

He opened up to Colonel Swamy while sipping on his cup of filter coffee. He wanted to learn operating computers. Knowing that it wouldn't be of much use to him at his age. 'Krishna should advise him about what to do.'

Colonel Swamy was so excited and shook Jaswant Babu's shoulders so hard that he dropped the plastic cup of coffee.

'Never mind.'

'It is a good idea, Mr Singh.' He poured him coffee in the cap of the thermos and said, 'If you want to learn, learn. Do it for your own happiness, not for usability.'

He gave his own example to encourage.

'Is this my age to learn music? Tell me.

'And classical at that?

'I wanted to learn, so I am.'

He surprised Jaswant Babu by telling him that Madhavi is a famous Carnatic singer. She is a well known name in the country's Carnatic music circuit. She has put her outstation performances on hold because of familial responsibilities. She keeps practising though. Wakes up at the crack of dawn for *riyaaz* and sits with her tanpura. She must have decided that the day Shreenivasan and Shreedharan get married, she will hand over her responsibilities to their wives and surrender herself to music.

'Do you know who my teacher is? Madhavi. Who else could have been a better teacher?'

He had ceremoniously offered her paan, supari, a coconut and eleven rupees as fee. She takes regular lessons. She sits with him in the afternoon.

Colonel Swamy sang a carnatic piece, starting with an aalap, on Jaswant Babu's request and Jaswant Babu felt like someone had pulled at his heartstrings. He found himself immersed in the music for a while even after the song was over. He didn't understand the meaning. But the notes had found their way into his heart.

'*Om laale Kandu Aaan.*' He remembered the opening lines of the song. This was the first time Colonel Swamy had mentioned his late wife.

'Vaidehi had asked Madhavi to sing this song on her deathbed. Madhavi sang with her eyes closed. Vaidehi listened with her eyes half open. Didn't realise she was seeing us for the last time.'

Colonel Swamy choked up. Or maybe Jaswant Babu was mistaken.

He had also felt a lump forming in his throat.

He had left Narendra's mother under Sunguniya's care and rushed to get the Doctor from Ashok Nagar.

She had passed away by the time he got back.

Narendra's mother had woken him up at four in the morning. Had complained of a really bad backache. It kept coming in spasms from the left side spreading to her left arm. She couldn't even lie in bed. He didn't know what to do at this time of the night. He took out a Combiflam from the medicine box and told her to swallow it with a glass of water. Rubbed Volini wherever she gestured him to rub. Decided to take her to the doctor as soon as he woke up. He started asking her if the pain was subsiding after giving her the pill. 'Is it gone? Should I call the doctor?' Rubbing the Volini did seem to comfort her a bit. After a minute she rued that she had unnecessarily ruined his sleep. She would have gotten up and taken the pill herself but the shooting pain stopped her. He should sleep. She was now comfortable.

At dawn, as the chirping of the birds on the banyan tree woke him up, he glanced at Narendra's mother who was deep asleep. He felt reassured. Couldn't have slept had the pain persisted. He was certain that Narendra's mother must have eaten rice yesterday night. She never felt sated without having rice for both her meals. She had come up with a new way to have rice, which she couldn't because of her diabetes. She would soak a few methi seeds with the rice. She also ate bitter gourd pickle all year round. How could her sugar go up? Her acidity might bother her at night but that didn't give her pains. He had tried reasoning with her. But she refused to listen to him. It was certainly flatulence and gastric trouble.

When Sunguniya came to sweep the verandah, he told her to get his lemon tea. Narendra's mother hadn't slept well at night because of the back pain. She should boil the milk too. He'll tell her he boiled it.

Narendra's mother didn't let Sunguniya touch the stove.

When Narendra's mother didn't wake up till sunrise, he got a little worried, kept the newspaper aside and called out to her.

His call was not answered. Narendra's mother's sleep has never been this deep! He touched her forehead. Shook her face. She stayed whichever side he turned her. Drooping.

Doctor Saxena gave up as soon as he arrived. Diabetics invariably have silent attacks. Unlike other heart patients, they don't get unbearable chest pains so that they can warn people around them.

Narendra was vocal in his anger about how he had behaved like an ignorant fool. He should have rushed her to the hospital as soon as she had complained of the pain. Why did he wait till the morning?

Jaswant Babu just kept staring into nothingness.

What would Narendra know! Old age could really make a fool of a man and his foolishness had just started.

He had admitted to Narendra's mother in a moment of weakness. She had raised her sisters-in-law with him. She had borne the brunt of his temper and demands. She is very strong. He was spoilt, couldn't live alone with his vices. He wanted her to die after him. That was the only course open to him and his dignity. He had tried many a times to gather the courage to confess to her about his character flaws. She is quarrelsome but large-hearted. She will definitely forgive him. He could never get himself to actually do so. Could not gather the courage to see himself falling in her eyes.

He also realised how foolish he had been to think, in his rashness that he'd live peacefully after her death. He was mistaken thinking thus. And he had lived all his life in that illusion.

He can't forget it. Narendra, the one to always profess undying love for his mother, refused to get his *mundan* done for her funeral because of work. What's there in hair? He didn't believe in rituals. There are people coming from abroad for a company visit. He'd go to Delhi after the *Chautha*. Will come back on the morning of the *Terahvin*. He had started fretting over him too or maybe he was just pretending to show concern keeping in mind the occasion. What will he do all alone after the *Terahvin*? Leave for Delhi with Narendra Bhaiyya – is what Shalini and Chauhan Babu opined.

Will think about it later. He'll let Narendra know. They shouldn't worry about food, he'll manage. He'll pay Sunguniya more and ask her to leave the work in one of her houses. She'll cook up something. They'll survive. That was his reply.

Jaswant Babu had made up his mind. His dependence on Sunguniya had rankled Shalini.

'Let's hire a cook, Babuji.'

He didn't reply.

'I can ask Pande Aunty next door. She'll find you someone.'

That was when Ahluwalia ji reassured her.

'*Guddi*, why are you so worried! We will send food over, for your Babuji.'

He had barely recovered from the funeral that he got another shocking news. Left him shaken.

He received news that his childhood friend Harihar Dubey had died.

Harihar had a bungalow with two bedrooms and a hall, made in the old style on Birhana road and had named it 'Mangal Bhavan.' He had returned a month ago from Kolkata where he had gone to his younger son, Aditya, for a cataract operation. He had called as soon as he reached back to Kanpur. He expressed his grief over the death of Narendra's mother. He was opening the house after a long time. There were bats hanging from the walls. He'll visit after getting the house cleaned. Bolstered him. He knew everything. When his wife Kaushalya had died, none of the four sons had passed 7th standard. How much does a clerk at PWD get paid? He gave tuitions. Cooked. Taught the kids. Took care of the house. At least, he didn't leave any of his responsibilities unfulfilled.

Aditya wasn't letting him leave. He had to fight him to come back. He wanted to spend some time doing some pooja. He'll leave for Kalpasan as soon as it is time for Kumbh.

Three days later the gate had to be knocked down.

The smell reached the neighbours then. Nobody knew when he came and when he left.

Harihar's corpse was found under the bed. One hand on the chest. Post-mortem report said it was a strong heart attack. He had gotten up from the bed to unlatch the door and died on the spot.

Jaswant Babu did not get to meet him one last time. The post-mortem had turned Harihar into a bundle of stench. He didn't want to see stench instead of his friend Harihar.

Disrupting memories of Harihar, the gut wrenching odour, didn't let him sleep for days. The smell had stuck to his nose and was refusing to go away. He had to keep an agarbatti lit every day. He would keep a roll of perfume-soaked cotton wad in his ears when he stepped out. Doctor Saxena was worried for him. Why was his blood pressure so high? It was not getting under control despite the medication.

Doctor Saxena got him to attend six sessions with psychiatrist Doctor Dutta, only then did he feel healthy.

The psychiatrist analysed all his problems. It was a minor psychological issue. Actually, the smell is nothing but fear. The fear of being lonely. He needed a change. He should stay at his son's in Delhi for a few days. Not just for a few days, he should stay there! He should not be staying alone at this age. Only those who have nobody to look after them should stay alone.

It was for this reason that Jaswant Babu could not call Narendra out of hesitation.

He called his daughter Shalini in Trivandrum instead. Talked to his grandchildren. The drops of their joy revived him. Then, he informed Shalini that his BP has been high lately. Doctor Saxena is worried for him. He is of the opinion that he should stay in Delhi.

'I had tried telling you this before, Babuji, but you didn't pay heed. Have you found someone?'

Babu Jaswant Singh cut the call as if the line had gotten disconnected.

A little later, Narendra called him. 'Babuji, pack your things, I am coming to pick you up next week.'

# Yeh Kya Jagah Hai, Doston!*
## (What Sort of a Place is this, Friends?)

Jaswant Babu was not in a state of indecision for too long. The time had passed. The clock had struck the designated hour. There was no hope of Colonel Swamy coming now. He also thought that walking was extremely important for his health and he should leave for the Pontoon Bridge alone and if Colonel Swamy meets him there, he'll scold him. Why didn't you come to walk? Did you not go for walks before our friendship? On top of that, he also felt that his blood pressure was probably high. He kept waking up at night. He kept thinking it was morning already. The dark told him it was still time to sleep. He should sleep. The morning will wake him up. He needs to get his BP checked as soon as the alarm goes off. He should get it checked every fifteen days but the exorbitant fee of Doctor Anurag Chaturvedi proves a deterrent. Doctor Anurag always spoke to him very sweetly because

---

* The reference is to the opening line of a song from Muzaffar Ali's film, *Umrao Jaan* that alludes to the feeling of strangeness and alienation in a place that should actually be familiar.

he knows Narendra. So sweetly that you'd think that the same tongue could not discuss fees. But as soon as it was time to go, he'd shatter the illusion and count the hundred fifty rupees of the fee unashamedly. The fee for getting your pressure checked in Kanpur is just five rupees. It was then that he felt that doctors such as Doctor Saxena were indeed a rare breed. His fee would go up or down depending on the paying capacity of the patient. He was unmatched in diagnosis and treatment in all of Kanpur.

His attention was suddenly diverted to the new flyover built in Nizamuddin. The street lights were still on.

❖

Yesterday, when he had reached home Sunayana had confronted him.

'Babuji, you forget to switch off the light in your room every day.'

'Might have forgotten.' Jaswant Babu's voice had broken while replying. But Sunayana did not pay attention to the break, the catch in his voice.

'The electricity meter doesn't stop running because of your forgetfulness,' she taunted.

He kept silent. Could he use his age as an excuse for asking for reprieve? If he could, would he not have got it without asking for it.

Narendra had said this when he was leaving after his mother's funeral.

There are two rooms in the flat, Babuji. We use one of them. The children use the other. There are two balconies of which one is fairly big – he might remember. He is going to get a darkened sliding glass put in it to close it off. That will become the children's room before he moves to Delhi.

Jaswant Babu had been surprised when he saw Narendra's office driver putting his luggage in the room that had been converted from the balcony.

He had mumbled that they'd be inconvenienced by his frequent bathroom visits in the night when Narendra offered a solution promptly – the balcony has a toilet. He needs a commode and the commode is there. The children's room has expensive gadgets and gizmos as also their computers. Those things can't be removed from there. In addition, the children's writing desk, books, cupboards and bunk beds are also in that room.

❖

As soon as you opened the sliding windows to the hot winds, you could see the naked balcony of the third floor of the house on Building B opposite. In the balcony, the drying clothes on the wires. A few that were worn by women but he had never seen them drying in the lanes of Kanpur. And there were a few huge aluminium trunks. Coolers one on top of each other. A long broom to remove cobwebs and a random assortment of other junk and clutter, the sight of which would always dishearten him. He'd feel like he was also thrown away in a corner like a piece of junk.

When reality hit Jaswant Babu after a long time, he consoled himself with the sight of the sliver of sun tying the two buildings and kite-shaped piece of blue sky in front of him. He used to sleep in the drawing room when he had visited earlier. He could still sleep there but it wasn't a matter of a few days any more. Setting yourself up in the drawing room was not very aesthetically pleasing.

The first morning, his sleep had just deepened when the lady of the house opposite started screaming to wake her servant up, in a way that could have challenged Indra's throne. He could not go back to sleep. The naughty servant was no less. He'd never wake up without having tried the mistress's patience. He wanted to go to the window and hurl abuses at that nincompoop. Hit him with his shoes for ruining the sleep of the neighbours.

The neighbour covered his view in such a way that his sliver of sun and the kite-shaped piece of sky were lost to him.

It was just about to be dawn and before five she would start blocking the view.

It had started almost that day too. Jaswant Babu was reading the morning newspaper, *Hindustan Times.* Benazir Bhutto was in Delhi and the headline sourced from the special Star TV programme 'Star Talk' was: 'Pervez planned Kargil when I was PM'. He couldn't find the time to read the papers. He had to wait for the others to have read it first. He felt relieved from ennui while reading the news.

Benazir's verbosity, though entertaining, could not but make him wonder why Benazir had not been this brave while still in power, when the doorbell rang. Jaswant Babu opened the door only rarely. Either Sunayana would get it or the children. He didn't open the door because he didn't always know the guests. Who he should call in, whom to keep out – was not a small dilemma.

'Babuji, you should have invited Chadha ji inside.' He was told as soon as Chadha ji left.

The second bell forced him to get up.

Sunayana was probably fast asleep.

He found the neighbour who had been threatening Indra's throne, when he opened the door. He invited her in and went to the children's room. Malay and Nilay were engrossed in playing car racing on the computer with their joysticks. He didn't like it that they were so involved in the game that they couldn't hear him. He only said this much. 'Go, wake your mother up. The aunty from the building opposite ours has come over.'

He turned back and found himself focused on the report on Benazir. But he was a little distracted while reading it.

He could hear that the neighbour and Sunayana were not talking but fighting vociferously. It was probably a Society-related issue. The members traded insults and accusations often. Sometimes over parking charges and sometimes over the 1½ percent hike in maintenance. The complaint was also that most of the members didn't attend the General Body Meeting and would air their disapproval only after a proposal was passed. The meetings to discuss the inaction of the committee always took place on Sundays at ten. The members would be sleeping till ten, enjoying their lazy Sundays. Narendra is a committee member, he had heard from Sunayana.

Jaswant Babu was shocked when after the neighbour's departure, Sunayana walked into his room and started screaming at him.

Why is Babuji so bent on ruining their reputation in the society? He should act according to his age. If he was still active like in his younger days, then what is the problem? He should go to the red-light area. It is not like his pension was small that he couldn't have some fun? At least, he should spare the young girls around. Allow them to save face in the society.

Jaswant Babu, dumbstruck, somehow managed to utter, 'What happened? What did I do?'

'What did you do? Don't you know?'

'How will I know if you don't tell me?'

'You ... You didn't loosen your pajama when you saw our neighbour Mrs Rawat's daughter?'

Blood rushed to his ears when he heard the accusation.

'I am old enough to be her grandfather. Why would I stoop so low?'

'That's something you'd know. Mrs Rawat had come to complain about this and has even told me to tell my colourful father-in-law to change his attitude or we will send a written complaint to the Society.

'She has also said that she'll even go to the police if need be.'

'Trust me, I haven't done anything so ill-begotten …' His voice suddenly carried a note of his earlier arrogance.

'Enough, Babuji. No need to explain yourself. Stop getting into these scrapes. It is worth thinking about, why would a mother complain about an old man? What is the need?

'And her daughter, Neena, what score does she have to settle with you?'

Shaking with anger, Sunayana hurled her accusations and left the room.

Jaswant Babu could not understand who he should explain himself to! He had been labelled a criminal without him having committed any crime. It was a strange situation. His own family was not willing to hear him out.

It isn't that Jaswant Babu had not seen the neighbour's daughter. He had seen her drying clothes or while picking them up. Whenever he saw that innocent girl he'd think that had Narendra had a daughter the house might have been livelier and not as dry as now.

He took off his glasses with shaking hands, then leaned against the headboard and lay in bed lifelessly. Once it almost felt like his head was spinning like the racing tyres of a car. Maybe today his head would come off his body. Good riddance. He will be free of all grief, unhappiness, complaints.

Would Sunayana have talked like this to her father?

No room for discussion. He was pronounced guilty.

He stuffed his spinning head into the pillow and started bawling like a baby. The metal bed started shaking with his sobs.

At dark, Narendra, who would step into his room every day, the room he had finally started acknowledging as a room, did not ask, 'Babuji, how was your day?'

Nilay came and kept the evening tea. There were four Marie biscuits on the side. 'Dadu, drink your tea,' was all he said. No warmth in his address. Wouldn't the children have heard the fight?

Tommy started growling when he saw him lying in bed. There was a difference in the growl. A curiosity. As if in spite of being an animal, only he had any sympathy for him.

What bothered him was why Tommy's leash was so short. Had it been longer, he knew he would have reached out and touched his feet with his paws – get up, won't you take me out for my evening round?

He refused to have dinner, completely ignoring Nilay's schooled request.

Jaswant Babu felt disheartened by the lack of sleep. Getting sleep didn't seem to be a problem for those who seemed to be bent on disappointing him in every which way.

He couldn't set the alarm that night. But he got up exactly at his usual time.

Unlike other days, Colonel Swamy was present on the Mayur Vihar flyover already. He stood there with his arms open to welcome him.

'What's wrong?'

'Let's sit.'

'Life is only lived fighting, Mr Singh,' Colonel Swamy tried to explain to him.

Jaswant Babu had tried to cover his face with his hands trying to hide his turmoil. He didn't want to break down in front of Colonel Swamy.

How many struggles could one face? Only Colonel Swamy could think this way and say something like this. He was far away from recriminations and humiliations. He couldn't imagine the hurt felt by the trunk of an old tree when it is hacked by a saw. He was treated so well by his sons, daughters-in-law and grandchildren. His walls resound with joy. And then there is him who kept dreaming that his grandchildren will play in his Kanpur house. Scribble on the walls. Draw stick figures on them. Create trees and flowers, the colours filled into which would spread all over the house. The disappointed faces would send him back to the market if he came back empty-handed.

It didn't take Colonel Swamy much time to realise that whatever had happened, was not minor. That there had been attempts to demolish him. The jibes of outsiders didn't hurt that much.

'Let's go sit somewhere first. We can walk later.'

They got off at the corner before the Pontoon flyover and sat on the sandy shores of Yamuna. Ignoring the dried flowers and polythene in the stagnant waters of the shores, Colonel Swamy laid a hand on his shoulder.

'What happened? I have never seen you so distraught.'

'….'

'Please talk … keeping your troubles bottled up inside will only fester them. It will hurt more.'

There was absolute silence between them for a while.

'The woman in Building B across my room came and complained to Sunayana … I took off my pajamas on seeing her daughter.'

Colonel Swamy let out an 'oh' as soon as he heard the words.

'I didn't do that … I can't do that…'

Colonel Swamy turned towards him. 'How did this misunderstanding happen?'

'Thought about it a lot. Then I remembered. Maybe the sliding windows of the room had been left open. I have always had constipation. Have to put a tube. Right then …'

'Did you tell your daughter-in-law the truth?'

'She wasn't willing to listen to anything.'

'I suggest, Mr Singh, that you should go to the neighbour's house. What is the most she'd do? She won't trust you. Let her.'

'….'

'Why should you live with the weight?'

'Why should I live at all?

'What if Narendra and Sunayana don't like it?'

Suddenly Jaswant Babu changed the topic and asked Colonel Swamy a strange question – what did he think of death?

Meaning to draw him out of his disturbed state of mind, Colonel Swamy said in a way to elicit a loud laugh – he didn't think of death at all. Let death come when it will. In whichever way it does. Whether it makes you suffer for a week, a month, a year or just whisks you away. Let it. But thinking of the suffering of those few days and becoming half-dead over it was making a mockery of life, wasn't it?

'Sir, live like a lion … the way you want, on your own terms.' Colonel Swamy pulled Jaswant Babu's cold hands into his warm fists.

When they got up from there, the morning-kissed kaash flowers stroked Jaswant Babu silkily.

Returning back from the pontoon flyover, Jaswant Babu felt that he wasn't alone. Colonel Swamy had been with him. Was still with him.

# Hide and Seek

Jaswant Babu bumped into Narendra, as soon as he entered home, who promptly chastised him.

Startled, he came back to earth. Colonel Swamy, who had accompanied him from his walk, was not with him anymore.

'Babuji, you left the lift door open on our floor?'

'Actually, I forgot to pick up my muffler while leaving for my walk. It was just for a few seconds. I thought I'd take it back soon. Why, did anyone say anything?'

'Forget about who said what. Keep this in mind, Babuji. The ones on the floor above might get inconvenienced. All you have to do is press a button and the lift will come back up.'

Jaswant Babu was distracted. His return made Tommy keep wagging his tail but that didn't comfort him in any way. His heart was aflutter while unlacing his shoes. Everybody was picking on him. So what if the lift reached a few minutes late? How was it such a big deal?

Nobody complained about the children in this house, only the aged. As if the people in this society will never get old. Neither their strength will diminish nor their mind. They are born so invincible that they will suffer no illness, no discomfort.

'Must have complained to Narendra or he wouldn't have known.' He didn't mutter but said aloud as if to someone, 'Not like he dreamt it up.'

As far as Jaswant Babu knew his morning routine – since he moved to Delhi, while Jaswant Babu savoured his morning tea, Narendra would be on his computer, checking emails and sending their replies. He was in regular contact with his friends working abroad. Shalu had mentioned once that Narendra had been trying to find a job in some company in America. Most of his friends from IIT were living lives of luxury abroad and making lakhs of money. Unfortunately, he was the only one left behind. He didn't want to lag behind anymore.

It was large hearted of Jaswant Babu that he accepted the truth, without any hesitation, that dealing with the lift was so difficult. Narendra wouldn't know. It wasn't possible for him to get up that early.

In the morning the lift was only used by the newspaper man, milkman, maids and car washers getting car keys from the houses. Everyone wants their newspaper as soon as they wake up and the newspaper men were much concerned about it. Whichever floor they were distributing newspapers on, they'd stop the lift there. The milkmen did the same thing. The maids and servants have a monopoly over the lift. Narendra doesn't even know that many a times, he'd give up on using the lift after calling for it repeatedly and use the stairs instead. Tommy didn't like him taking the stairs. He would refuse to budge from near the lift. On top of that, the Society members are also strange. All their anger gets directed at the senior citizens. They don't realise that the lift is needed more by the old than the young. Owners more than servants. Although he shouldn't think like this. They too are human. But the truth is also that he has never complained about it to either his family or to the society members that the lift is usually not available for use in the mornings.

In spite of his anger, it did occur to Jaswant Babu that he was only thinking of himself. How will people realise these things? They couldn't see the old in the society.

Before he met Colonel Swamy, didn't he also keep looking for people his age? Except for Mr Bhatt in Building 'C', he hadn't come across any other old person. He would meet Mr Bhatt only in the evenings and exchange pleasantries. Mr Bhatt told him about himself. Morning walks didn't agree with him. Especially in winters. He only stepped out in the evenings. Evenings start at four for him. He only walked in the park in the neighbourhood. It was impossible to go too far. It was too dangerous. Why should he take such a risk?

Mr Bhatt informed him that sometime earlier all the senior citizens from the societies nearby (Kala Vihar, Manas, Nirman, Vardhaman, Samachar, Keerti, etc.)

had gotten together and formed a laughing club. To stay healthy. They would get together in the park at eight in the morning and practise laughing loudly. The laughing club ran successfully for a couple of months to a couple and a half. The youngsters taking morning walks couldn't stand the demonic 'Hahas' of these old people with their sagging skins and dentures. Their reasoning was that it felt less like laughter, more like a roar. How long could they stand this feeling? The opposition started. If you want to laugh, go laugh in your homes. The park is a public place. What if they started wailing loudly tomorrow arguing that crying is good for the health, how could they bear that? The old got scared. They met the next morning but didn't laugh.

Best to not get into an argument with the young. So they changed the laughing club into a prayer meeting. The change in the programme resulted in a change in the timing. By forenoon, the park would get abandoned. Now, one of them would fish out a tape-recorder from his pocket and Asaram Bapu's teachings would get played over it.

The old would listen to the teachings and try to move beyond worldly pleasures.

They kept listening to Asaram Bapu and some of the old people died. Their place was taken by the newly-minted old.

'I am also waiting for my turn, Mr Singh. Whenever the divine one ordains it.' Mr Bhatt raised his arms to the skies, as if not praying to the god above but asking for death.

Every time Mr Bhatt bumped into Jaswant Babu, he never forgot to request him to join them for their prayer meetings.

If he wants, he can even come and pick him up from his home.

Initially, his heart had fluttered.

Familiarity had stopped him because contact with any society member was not good for him. Who knows when his mouth would open and all his complaints might reach Sunayana's ears. Will it take any time for his court-martial?

The tea had been soured so much that it was difficult for him to even take a sip. Looks like the fridge is flush with lemons.

Had Narendra's mother made such a mistake, Jaswant Babu would have flung the tea in the drain.

Till the time the tea leaves put in boiling water didn't give the colour of *Old Monk* rum and the lemon drops put in it after didn't give it a golden tinge, the tea wouldn't go down his throat. Sunayana didn't learn anything from her perfectionist mother-in-law. She is only good at one thing – taming her husband.

Like a burst of vinegar, the sour tea reminded him of a hated incident.

He was still convinced that Sunayana has some superpower making her so good at brainwashing Narendra.

Narendra had promised a long time ago that he'd fulfil Babuji and Ammaji's wish of visiting Badrinath and Kedarnath. That he won't visit Kedarnath otherwise. He was trying to eke out a week from his busy schedule. Narendra couldn't find the time and his mother left them.

Narendra informed him as soon as he could free up some time. It was in September. He had suddenly planned a trip to Kedarnath with his friends. They'd all drive down in their cars with their respective families. The children will have to take leave.

He had to check with his friends in spite of deciding to take him along. It wasn't advisable to take him to Kedarnath at his advanced age. You could reach Badrinath by car, no problem. The difficulty is in getting to Kedarnath. Scaling a height of thirteen kilometres was no laughing matter. Oxygen was also low at the top. The bone-chilling cold might even result in pneumonia. There were no arrangements for emergency situations in Kedarnath. Accidents were heard of too often. The aged falling off cliffs along with their palanquins. Finding the bodies had become difficult.

He will have no trouble living here alone. They had spoken to the trusted peon of his office.

His younger brother Shyamsaran will live with him all day here for a week. He is an expert in cooking on gas. Shyamsaran was always taken as the cook on office picnics.

They'll put Doctor Anurag Chaturvedi's home and clinic numbers on the calendar and show it to him. He should call him if there was any need. Narendra will personally tell Doctor Anurag that he is leaving Babuji here in his care.

'If you still want to go …'

Jaswant Babu felt his entire body go up in flames.

He was being asked for his opinion after the entire programme had been decided upon. That too after sealing his lips! He was amazed at his own forbearance.

He'll have to agree. Shravan Kumar was relegated to legends and story books.

It was Colonel Swamy who had taken him sight-seeing in Delhi. Narendra has a Zen which is used to pick up and drop his wife's relatives, visiting from abroad, from the airport and to take them around. It was only for him that Narendra could not find the time. Why should he even bother about it?

If he ever mentioned to Colonel Swamy that he wanted to visit Badrinath-Kedarnath, he'd draw up a plan immediately and tell him to pack his things.

He had just mentioned in passing that he hadn't seen a movie in the last seven years. Colonel Swamy informed him three days later. 'Reach Glaxo flyover at exactly quarter to two in the afternoon today.' They are going to Delite Cinema to watch *Aks*. He really likes Raveena of the *mast-mast* fame. The eldest son got two balcony tickets yesterday on his way from work.

Impulse suddenly took over. He'd call 197, give Colonel Swamy's landline number to the operator and ask for his address and ask them why he wasn't being able to get through to this number.

197 told him that the landline number was working fine. Maybe there wasn't anyone home. Please note down the address – E-303, Sector 26, Noida.

The phone was working fine but nobody was answering it. What did that mean?

Fear took over like a broken record. The absence of the entire family was inexplicable. How was it possible?

Colonel Swamy has a *Jonga*. He had mentioned it. He had also said that he didn't drive the car. If he had to go to a party, such as to the Army Officer's Club, he called a taxi. It freed him up to drink. If the family was going somewhere, they'd take the *Jonga*. It is a nice car. Only a *Jonga* could fit in so many people. They'd climb on top of each other, squabble, play *Antakshari*, impersonate Annu Kapoor, make fun of Boogie-Woogie, blame Doordarshan for the degradation of culture and blame government policies to let it happen – their faces would fall on reaching the destination. Reached already? Hadn't they just left? This was bad. Shyamali would get disappointed. There was no choice. They had come to watch a movie and that too at Chanakya. They'd have to listen to Anu Malik's deafening film songs inside the theatre. They'd be deprived of lilting music that'd remove the difference between Shyamali the Great's singing and the wailing. 'Shyamali, my darling! No need to feel sad. You will be given a chance to showcase your bad singing in the Great Jonga Show on the way back. You will sing, right?'

Shyamali would roll her eyes at her mischievous husband and complain to him, 'Appu, please tell him to stop making fun of me. Enough is enough.'

Hope the *Jonga* didn't get into an accident?

Uff! Babu Jaswant Singh bit his tongue with his teeth.

❖

'You have to drink, friend ...'

'What will you drink?

'No, no, you can't discuss all this fasting and rituals in front of me.

'Admitted, you have quit drinking but how does it matter if you start again today after so long? Start again and see!'

Colonel Swamy requested him from across the table and smiled.

'Do you know, drinking alcohol after a long time is as exciting as meeting an old flame.'

Both of them were sitting in the bar above the Nirula's in Noida.

Bathed in the mystique of low lights that didn't let you study the face sitting across.

Roasted salty peanuts that Jaswant Babu had been craving for and was eating after a very long time – chewing with his only strong molar, he worried that he wasn't being able to control his greed. He will have to face indigestion tomorrow morning.

Colonel Swamy had ordered his favourite whiskey, *Royal Challenge* and a Bloody Mary for him.

Colonel Swamy had fixed it up with him in the morning. He was getting bored of drinking alone at home and wanted to have dinner and drinks with Jaswant Babu in the Noida Nirula's. He will take a taxi and pick him up from the Glaxo Apartments gate. He'll call him before leaving. Mr Singh should come down in twelve minutes. He shouldn't worry about returning. He'll drop him.

Narendra hadn't returned home yet. The children were engrossed in watching the CD of 'Aladdin' on their computer, after having practised skating in the basement. Sunayana was in a bad mood. She was scolding the children. They should leave the computer and finish their homework first. He had to inform Sunayana that he will be going out and will not eat at home. That he is going to Noida Nirula's. Sunayana almost ignored him and said in an angry tone. The bloody spots on his pajamas and underwear do not come off in the washing machine. A slab of Rin detergent bar has been kept in his bathroom. He should wash off the spots before putting the clothes in the washing machine. The children's uniforms have starting yellowing because of his carelessness.

Babu Jaswant Singh got a little miffed.

This wasn't the time for such a conversation. He could have been told later how to manage the effects of this sickness that bothered him so! Sunayana probably could not stand his excitement.

Blood has started coming out with farts. Clothes get filled. He was also exasperated. What she is saying is right. But what should he do? He is taking his medicines, putting the tube. He was scared of getting operated upon. The matter, in spite of being serious, was being ignored. He was ignoring it.

Colonel Swamy had given a suggestion. He should get some sanitary napkins. Use them like women do. Instructions for usage are given on the packet. The situation would get under control to a great extent.

Jaswant Babu couldn't stop laughing on hearing the suggestion. Then, taking a dig at himself, he said – this was the only thing left, this would also get checked out.

The suggestion seemed to have its merits. He called up Arora Chemists next morning, asking for the pads. How many packets? Neither Colonel Swamy had an estimate nor he. Let's ask the chemist. Talking to Sunayana about this issue would be futile. He still remembers. Some medicines had gotten over. He told Sunayana he needed them. She had given him the contact number for Arora Chemists. He can order them over phone. He'll deliver the medicines home and take the money.

It had rankled Jaswant Babu. Sunayana feels Babu Jaswant Singh draws a hefty pension. He should spend it instead of hoarding.

Sons are bank accounts for fathers – isn't Sunayana's husband his bank account?

It is a different matter that he does have money. He spends it too. Before asking Narendra for it. He feels that he should contribute too. He always got something for Malay-Nilay every time he stepped out. He was also very fond of 'Milk Treat'. He ate his share as soon as he stepped out of the shop.

Colonel Swamy ordered a second peg for Jaswant Babu and himself.

'By the way, alcohol and girlfriends remind me, Mr Singh ... have you ever been in love? Other than the wife one.' Colonel Swamy said that in a hushed tone and laughed a silent laugh.

Jaswant Babu felt that it wasn't the Bloody Mary but Colonel Swamy's question that had suddenly made him think of Shivani.

The heat of fast, steaming breaths started spreading through his mangled heart like fire.

He was amazed – the heart never grows old!

Jaswant Babu steadied himself. Almost as if he had just separated Shivani from himself and merely turned sides.

He also felt that the colonel wanted to share some secrets of his own on the pretext of asking about Jaswant Babu's.

'You tell me about yourself.'

'I?' Colonel Swamy seemed a little uncomfortable. Took a large sip from the glass. He didn't take a second to gulp it down his throat.

'Yes, you!' Jaswant Babu felt that his guess wasn't wrong. A smile was flowering on the Colonel's lips.

'I … I am immersed in the last love of my life. In silence. Not letting anyone know. Someday I'll blast a bomb like at Pokhran. Flooring everyone at home. I am a little impatient to introduce my Giligadu to this love. My Love is also getting impatient, my friend. You have also been mentioned.'

'It has been said, you are lucky, Colonel! I envy you …'

Colonel Swamy has been exchanging letters with Mumbai's Anima Das.

Colonel Swamy is trying to understand Anima Das and Anima Das wants to understand him. The thousands of miles between them is getting shrunk in their letters by some measure. Measure by measure, they were trying to traverse the distance and they were both confident that they would soon cross the distance between them. In fact, conquer it. Both of them also felt that they should get to know each other well so that when they meet, they don't act like strangers. They should know each other's faces and each and every facet of their personalities. They had each counted the number of moonshine greys in their hair. They didn't want that the time they get to spend in each other's company gets wasted in getting to know each other. If that happens, Anima Das feels it'd be a waste of time. Both of them were eager to cross whatever little distance was left between them. Anima Das says that she'll measure her failings first with the scale used to measure distances. Those failings that had deleted the words from the lessons from her past.

Anima Das has a computer. Colonel Swamy also has a computer. They did talk to each other over emails but even in those few days, Anima Das realised that it is difficult to put yourself across in emails. Especially when one has to and desires to explain oneself entirely, such that one can feel fulfilled, complete after writing it. Anima Das deeply feels that her innocent, determined – never leaving anything incomplete, even her smaller letters could take her aim to its fulfilment. She'd expressed herself in those letters. You can tuck the letters under the pillows and sleep. Letters didn't weave themselves into dreams but into reality, in sleep. Anima Das felt that she was touching him by touching his writing in the letters. You can't sleep with the computer under your pillow! The computer has trapped the secrets of a lot of people. Letters alone are one's private space. It is one's own sky on one's own earth. Now, Anima Das wants her own space. Where no one other than herself could put their words.

A thick file of Colonel Swamy's letters was pilling up at Anima Das's place.

Colonel Swamy has also made a file of Anima Das's letters. Now, he has started feeling that he should meet her soon. How should the first meeting happen, where, alone or with the family around, hers or his – was yet to be decided.

Anima Das has sent pictures of herself. Black and white and in colour. On a soft looking face, there were three wrinkles under both her eyes. There was a fourth one forming under the right eye perhaps. There were two deep lines, almost as if cut by knife, on the corners of her smiling lips. On a plain forehead, two blurred lines appear, as if drawn by a foot ruler. The face would look grander with two more. A bindi absent on her forehead.

Colonel Swamy wrote to her with no hesitation. The blank forehead was changing her face into a symphony-like sombre tone. He couldn't stand it. He wants to see a big bindi on her forehead. Could she please do this for him?

Anima Das sent him a picture with a big bindi the very next week. On seeing the picture, Colonel Swamy felt that unlike in the previous colour photo there was a hint of lipstick on her lips in this one. Colonel Swamy felt drawn to Anima Das's glowing face.

Anima Das has written a poem in English for Colonel Swamy. She writes that without a moustache, his long face resembles a thin lane whose stony path puts people off from treading on it.

How long does it take for the moustache to grow back?

If he were to take her advice, he should immediately grow one. He should send her a photo from every stage of his growing moustache. They can meet only once his moustache has fully grown out. He should not worry about grooming his moustache. As such, he has a strong personality. If necessary, he could get it groomed in a salon. Also, the moustache should be turned up just like in his photo from the 1971 war with Pakistan.

Anima Das is very impressed with Colonel Swamy's previous pictures.

She writes – the way in which she was dying to see him, Colonel Swamy looked exactly that dashing in that picture.

Anima Das had written – she remembers that heart-wrenching incident he had written about, the sad phase that was the most challenging one in his life as a soldier. The moment when his brave friend, Colonel Samar Pratap Singh of the Gorkha regiment, posted at the Kutch Border, while pushing the Pakistani forces back, got turned into a lump of flesh by their cannon-balls. That was the moment he realised that. His friend had been martyred and he got saved like a coward because he wanted to be safe. Now, he will never keep a moustache. He had no right to keep a moustache. He had shaved it off as soon as they had returned from the border.

Anima Das had also written that the time for them to meet has arrived. Anima Das really likes Nainital. She wants to meet Colonel Swamy there for the first time. Hotel Classic faces Naini Lake. You can see Naina Devi Temple from its balcony. You can hear strains of the evening aarti from there. You can also see Sherwood School. You can see the reflection of the huge mountain in the large lake. She is booking two rooms in Hotel Classic for any of the dates in the last week of the next month, December. She will book them from Mumbai. She will inform him of the dates then. Colonel Swamy doesn't have to do anything. He just needs to reach Nainital with his woollens. Anima Das will reach Nainital via Delhi. She will stop at Delhi for a day, although not yet decided where to stay. Colonel Swamy will meet her for the first time in Delhi only. He should not worry. She will take care of everything in Nainital. And she will stay there till she wants to.

There was only a fortnight left for their meeting.

He will inform Madhavi, Anushree, Shyamali just when he is about to leave for Nainital.

He won't bother with trains or buses. He will rent a car. Anima Das has sent him a long poem. New. In the eight-page long poem, she has disclosed the date of their meeting in Nainital. 28th December! It could snow around that time. The new year also starts. No better days, he could think of, to be in Nainital.

Colonel Swamy was a little touched on receiving an eight-page long poem. A poem also creates a poem!

Colonel Swamy has brought along a photocopy of Anima Das's poem. To give to Mr Singh. He should read it once he gets home. He should tell him when they meet in the morning for their walk. What he thinks of his Anima Das's poetry!

How did it all begin? The slight blush on Colonel Swamy's face did not escape Jaswant Babu's notice in spite of the dim lighting.

What had happened was that Colonel Swamy had one Sunday after his morning walk, noticed a very interesting ad by one Anima Das in the Matrimonial section of *Times of India*. 'A pensioner widow reader is looking for a single or widower companion who would give her company in the last stage of life. Having gotten her son and daughter married off, she was free of all responsibilities. The children are busy with their familial obligations. And she was feeling lonely. Interested candidates should send their photograph with a CV.'

The ad had appealed to Colonel Swamy. More so, the woman's courage. A lot of people could judge her for this decision. Let them. He felt like she was someone like him. Colonel Swamy decided to exchange letters with Anima Das. He sent a family picture and a CV to the post box number mentioned. He has no qualms in accepting that he wasn't very serious while doing so. As per Anima Das's demands he was a widower but not alone. Neither was he bothered with loneliness in his big family.

Colonel Swamy was of course excited about the reply. After a while, he felt that maybe he had been unsuccessful in establishing his suitability. But in the fourth week of the month that was drowning him in despair, he received Anima Das's reply. Anima Das was very impressed with him. She wrote that she would like to keep in touch with him. She had met someone matching her wavelength after a long time. She was sending him her email id. Can he also please send her his email id?

❖

Had Colonel Swamy left for Nainital? Maybe their plan had changed and Anima Das might have informed him, over email to reach Nainital pronto.

But the family? The two had no connection. Maybe they decided to meet with family. And they left for Nainital with family. It is possible that he spends a few weeks there.

Maybe they felt that whatever decision they make about each other, they should do so in consultation with their families. So that there is no room for any dispute or unhappiness in future. That's fine. That's what should happen. Nothing to stop it from happening. Colonel Swamy is everyone's favourite Appu!

Sunayana is roaring – Babuji, will you eat at the dining table or in your room?

'I'll eat at the dining table.'

Jaswant Babu gets up to reach the dining table. He wanted to sit with the children. He was fine with Sunayana's roar.

Tommy was focussed on slurping off his milk and roti from his bowl. He crossed him on the way but Tommy didn't have the time to look up.

The visions had started moving. He was tired.

❖

His head was hurting. Could be because of the cold. He needed the room to be hot enough to make him sweat.

Where should he get it? After that humiliating incident, he hadn't opened the sliding windows till date. He could go downstairs to sun himself. There were a few benches in the Society's little garden. Some people used them too. He was the only one who couldn't. Among many other reasons was the fear that people sitting there might start whispering about the incident with the neighbour.

# Long Poem

In the afternoon, as soon as he had had his lunch, Jaswant Babu was in the habit of taking a nap. He had tried hard to leave the bed after lazing about for a bit. Sit on a chair. There were no chairs here, so just leaning against the headboard was enough. Try to read a book even if an old one but even books seem to be angry with him. He would barely leaf through a page or two that he'd start letting out a stream of yawns. He could read books only at night. Sleep's hide and seek would barely start and he'd sit with a book open in front of him. He'd start getting sleepy. He was grateful to Premchand and Rabindranath Tagore in this context for keeping him away from the habit of taking sleeping pills. Babu Jaswant Singh wasn't sure whether there were any writers from this part of the country who were this influential or eminent.

The lack of a solution for the dilemma of the afternoon was bothering him a lot. The sequence of endless burps that had started in Kanpur was not letting him sit in peace in Delhi. The sound of the bursting burps would disgust Sunayana to such an extent that she'd feel like throwing up.

The morning walks might have had some effect on his health but his stomach had refused to show any results. Jaswant Babu always ate in measured quantities. But even then he failed to understand what was weighing on the machinery of his stomach in such a way that it refused to function properly. In these times of trouble, he'd miss Narendra's mother. Whenever she'd step out to shop, she'd buy samples of whatever new digestives she could find in the market. Their effect would give him some relief for a few days.

Sunayana would want to shoot at him and if she couldn't do it herself she would rest the gun on Narendra's shoulders and take aim.

'Please take a stroll in the room after eating, Babuji.'

'Which room?'

'This is precisely your problem – you always misinterpret everything.'

'Will you never get old, Narendra?'

'It is not a question of old or young but a matter of adjustments.'

'Absolutely – can't you teach your wife this lesson? Shouldn't she learn how to live with elders? Sneezes, farts, burps don't consider age, Narendra. Anybody with bad digestion will face these issues.'

Narendra did not prolong the discussion and went back to his room. The loud sounds coming out of their room in spite of a closed door alienated him further in this house.

This time Jaswant Babu was walking around in the room, stroking his chest and neck while letting out burps.

Just then, Nilay knocked on his door to let him know he had a call. Jaswant Babu leapt at the phone joyously. Colonel Swamy has returned home?

He was disappointed to hear a panicky girl rambling over the phone. The girl said hello and immediately asked if she could talk to Jaswant Singh Tauji.

Tauji? Who could it be addressing him as Tauji? The girl was talking very respectfully.

'It is me, tell me?'

'Tauji! I am Sumitra from Kanpur, Netaji's eldest daughter. How are you?'

Netaji! Oh ho! Ram Khilawan Yadav's daughter. He remembered suddenly. He was overjoyed.

'I am fine, Beta,' Jaswant Babu replied. He realised he'd now be able to talk to Sunguniya.

Sunguniya took the phone. She started expressing her anger at his long absence as soon she heard his voice over the phone. Jaswant Babu asked her as soon as he could get the chance – why hadn't she called all these days? Sunguniya said this to express her inability. How could she? The phone could only be dialled by Netaji's eldest daughter away from the eyes of the other family members. She hadn't been in town. She had been in Lucknow for two-and-a-half weeks to choose a bride for the elder brother. Came back the previous morning. She dialled the number today and that is why she could talk to Master. Master should listen to her carefully. Master is miles away from her. Who should Sunguniya consult if she had to ask about right or wrong? There's no dearth of people around to give her wrong advice. One thing. Netaji has been after her life to get her to join his party.

Elections are going to be announced soon. Lower castes were being rallied to make the party stronger. The power of the Brahmins and Thakurs had to be upended. Only then will the lower castes get some dignity. Have to make their own destiny. Our party should come into power again.

Netaji is saying that Sunguniya should get a ticket for his party, BSP. He'll make her a member. Sunguniya will only have to work for the party as soon as she becomes a member. She'd have to go to the office regularly. The office is in Hulaganj. She'd have to commute. Netaji has also explained her duties. She'd have to sweep and mop the office. Have to offer water to all guests. Keep an eye on those who are critical of Netaji. Who is a traitor. Who is unsatisfied. Who is a backstabber. They'd think she is an ordinary woman and will not guard their tongue in her presence.

Netaji also said she'd have to go with Mistress to the slums to rally her caste-mates so that they get rallied. Brahmins and Thakurs have been raping their wives and daughters. Didn't let them succeed. Treated them like the soles of their shoes. Made them work without pay. Pissed in their mouths when they opened their mouths to ask for pay. Thrown their corpses in gutters. But all this will now stop. The days of the rule of Brahmins and Thakurs are over. Now we will rule and piss in the mouths of those imbeciles. Ten in one mouth!

According to Netaji, Sunguniya will have to leave all the houses she is working at. He is showing her dreams that he will arrange a house for her as soon as he gets elected. She'd never have to work for a Thakur again. She's not going to need their kindness. She'd have a house as soon as the slums around Swaroop Nagar get built. She'd draw a salary from the Party's office. Eleven hundred Rupees lumpsum! By the tenth of every month. There was another proposal by Netaji – that Sunguniya return to her husband's ancestral village in Birhun. Netaji will make her the head of the Gram Panchayat. Nobody will dare to question Netaji's selection.

When Sunguniya refused to go back to the village he asked her why she didn't want to go back there. She shouldn't worry about the children. He'll get them admitted into the school in the village. Sunguniya was forced to open her mouth in protest. Master should forgive her. There was no other option. She told Netaji in clear terms. She hadn't been harassed by Brahmins and Thakurs in her village. Her own family had. A woman is a woman even for family members. On the fifth night after her husband's funeral her elder brother-in-law had pounced on her. Warned her that if she made a sound, he'd throw her only son in the deep well outside the village. She got scared and kept her mouth shut. All this harassment wasn't enough. They got her marriage fixed overnight with an old idiot so that they didn't have to give her a share in the property.

Master is privy to all her struggles. Her goddess-like Mistress had taken her under her wing. She had taken Sunguniya to the police to file a report that if her eldest brother-in-law is ever seen anywhere near their house, he should be taken into custody.

Sunguniya told Netaji clearly. If it doesn't suit him, then so be it. She wants to raise her children in peace. Neither does she want to work in the Party office nor does she want to become a Panchayat Head in the village. She'd keep sweeping and mopping their house till the time they let her. She is grateful to him for getting her children admitted into schools. Master should tell whether Sunguniya had done the right thing by rejecting Netaji's proposal.

Babu Jaswant Singh got a little emotional while listening to Sunguniya. All he said was that he had never found Sunguniya's decisions wrong. He believed that she could never take a wrong decision. He wanted to speak his mind to Sunguniya. She shouldn't call him Master. What should she? Call him Babuji. She has addressed him as Babuji inadvertently on occasions, which he liked.

Jaswant Babu also knew that Sunguniya hadn't called him up for advice but to let him know of her decision. Sunguniya wasn't unaware of the kind of politicians who try to play on the weaknesses of the unprivileged. These people try to reap their own dreams by sowing dreams of peace in the minds of those with worries.

Jaswant Babu realised that he didn't ask about Ramvati-Somvati aka Katyayani and Kumudini as soon as he lay down. The agitated Sunguniya also didn't realise while crying hoarse about Ram Khilawan Yadav that he might want news of the children. That he might want to know what the children are being taught in school. How much have they learnt? Did they talk about it at home? Did they need copies, books or slates? If they did and if money was tight, he could send some money in Sunguniya's name by money order. The post office is far but not so far that he couldn't get there.

The best part was that Jaswant Babu had never asked Sunguniya's children to come to him. If he ever, even mistakenly called for them, they'd stand there, shrunken, with their heads bent. He had told Sunguniya to check why they were so scared of him. It hadn't occurred to him to make friends with them. He'd get something for them when he stepped out. They wouldn't come near him to take that either. Defeated, he'd have to give the chocolates or wafers to Sunguniya. Sunguniya took the initiative on seeing his desire fulfilled. Like they should go check in his room whether Master has woken up or not. Ask Master whether he needed tea. Go, get the newspaper from the doorstep for him. The whimpers of Ramvati aka Katyayini's hesitation started fading away. The other two would enter the room like her tail and run away as soon as she turned her back. As if there was a mad dog giving them chase. Dog – him, he … dog. The smile barely touched his lips that it blossomed into a momentary laugh. After so many days and in this house!

Jaswant Babu remembered that Katyayani should have gotten admitted last year and Kumudini this year. Ramratan is too small right now. Narendra's mother used to worry more about the girls. They could be seen jumping across the gates. She believed that if they went to school, they'd be away from home even if just for five-six hours. Had she been alive, she would have made sure Ramratan got into school too.

Narendra's mother had gone to the government school nearby for this very reason a number of times. The proceedings got halted because of their birth certificates. Where to get them from? They were born in the village. The Principal suggested that they get the birth date written by the Panchayat Head with a stamp by the Panchayat. That will do. Ramasre was alive then. He said, 'I am going to village for some work. Will get the Panchayat Head's stamp.' Sunguniya couldn't go to the village. The last recourse was the Magistrate. They were just about managing when Narendra's mother cheated them. It is different for Netaji. His influence could get things done easily.

Jaswant Babu started feeling sleepy.

Sunayana's voice woke him up a little later. Sunayana in his room? Was he dreaming? Dreams were no less strange. He had wet the bed till he had been much older. In his sleep, he'd think he was pissing in the urinal...

It was Sunayana indeed. She left his tea and two Marie biscuits in the small tray. The children must have gone to play downstairs.

Jaswant Babu liked it that she had come into his room. He didn't know whether she liked it or not. The biscuits had the crisp freshness about them. He had often felt that he was being sent the soggy, leftover biscuits. Sunayana probably felt that there was no better dustbin than him.

It didn't take long for an unexpected quarrel at dinner time when Narendra put his mind to it.

Narendra said that Sunayana had gone to the bank in the morning. She was saying that the rent for the locker has really gone up. Why isn't Babuji surrendering his locker in Kanpur? There is no point in needlessly paying rent. Anyway, there's no need for two lockers in the same family. It is difficult minding scattered things.

Narendra offered his services. If Babuji was in agreement, he could take leave on Saturday and they could leave for Kanpur. He knew that the bank was open on Sunday mornings. They'll wrap up the work in the morning and take the Shatabdi back in the evening. They will get the house opened and cleaned up by Sunguniya on Saturday on this pretext.

Sunayana also felt the same, and Narendra agreed with her, that mother's silk saris and expensive shawls could be rotting away in the cupboard because of lack of care. It is better if they get used. Sunayana will be happy to wear them. When Amma was alive, she had often requested Sunayana to wear them as her silk saris were of no use to her anymore. They belong to Sunayana now. She'd take them out for Sunayana before she leaves Kanpur. But Sunayana hadn't agreed. Her rationale was that Amma had a lot of social obligations in Kanpur. She could borrow the saris anytime.

Babuji should let them know his decision in the matter.

Jaswant Babu could not swallow the bite he had put in his mouth, stunned. He left the rest of the food and kept gulping down water. Trying to muster courage to talk. There was a time when he didn't have to look for courage within himself. How situations change, how indeed they have changed!

He finally opened his mouth. Sunayana and Narendra's eyes were pinned on him in anticipation of his reply.

Narendra … Narendra, your mother is not yet dead for me …' Jaswant Babu roared and got up from the dinner table.

Who are these people? Are they waiting for him to die? No, not even wanting to wait.

It's possible that while complaining to Colonel Swamy about Sunayana and Narendra, Colonel Swamy might end up talking about his whiny behaviour instead. He might say that not only is your son intelligent but also very practical. It is important to be practical when needed. Whatever is in the locker is after all thcirs. Whether it reaches them today or tomorrow, how does it matter! Who else but they have a right to their mother's things! They also know that these hold their mother's memories. Wear them, touch them, they'll feel their mother's presence. You should enjoy. Leave all these household matters be. You can't die with the dead, Mr Singh. It will be for the best if you stop dying with the dead. The children won't be able to live if they do. Live and let live.

Jaswant Babu won't be able to turn back and retort to Colonel Swamy, even if he wanted to, that his children were not like the colonel's children.

He also thought that Colonel Swamy will not be able to understand his mental agony since he didn't have to suffer a similar situation.

Is Jaswant Babu envious of Colonel Swamy's happiness? Does he think he should agree with him on everything? Should say what he wants him to say!

No, that's not true probably. Jaswant Babu does get irritated but he is not petty, or mean.

Where is Colonel Swamy? Where? He needs him so much right now. If he could meet him, he'd certainly feel calmer. Harihar Dubey has also left him…

Where is the photocopy of Anima Das's long poem? Where did he keep it? He looked for it in the papers under his pillow but couldn't find it. He had searched for it earlier too.

Jaswant Babu tried hard to remember. He was under the spell of a sweet passion, Colonel Swamy had said. He had especially gotten a copy done of Anima Das's long poem for him. He should read the poem and let him know his opinion the next morning for sure. How did he like the poem? How did Anima Das write?

He also remembered that when they met the next morning, he had asked him about the poem, 'Read it?' He had said that he couldn't find the copy in the pocket of his coat. Couldn't remember whether he had kept it elsewhere at night. Usually, he didn't empty his coat pockets. If he needed something, he'd take them out from the pocket. If he kept it anywhere else, the only safe place was under his pillow. Colonel Swamy got worried when he heard this. It is possible that he had said he'd give it to him but he forgot! Maybe Anima Das's long poem got left on that table in Nirula's! Now, he will perhaps not be able to photocopy Anima Das's long poem. That was a moment. The moment when he had felt that he should get the poem read by Mr Singh. He didn't know if that moment will ever come back or not. But even then, if he ever crossed paths with Anima Das's long poem, he should read it.

Why had his eyes gotten wet?

# Third Absence

# Dream

It was around eleven in the morning. That's what it seemed to Jaswant Babu in his deep sleep.

Around this time, all other members of the family except for Sunayana and Tommy are not at home. The house is quiet, the environment conducive for resting his tired legs after the long morning walk. Even if the walk hadn't been long, he tries not to break an old habit. This time as well, he was keeping the habit.

He knew that eleven was the time for Sunayana to be alert about everything. This was the time the housemaid, Sitabai, would be sweeping and mopping the floors and dusting the furniture. Sunayana had announced that she should not be asked to do anything else at this time. Even if she were asked, it will be difficult to follow through. She was of the opinion that cleaning time was when all good housewives should have their eyes trained on the house help. What if they with great deftness steal the kohl out of their mistress's eyes? It had happened a lot of times that after a week or so of engaging a maid, she has realised that some of her expensive things have gone missing. On asking Sitabai, she had turned around and questioned her. Did a crow call at her window? On being told that it cawed in the morning, Sitabai caught the thief immediately. The crow has made away with Madam's valuables. Has Madam never seen a vulture fly away with a snake in its beak? It will be better if Madam shuts all windows in the morning as soon as she hears the crows. Then she should see whether valuables disappear or not.

When Jaswant Babu heard of the incident he only said this much to Sunayana. What's the need of taking of jewellery off your ears and neck every night? He has never seen Narendra's mother doing that. Married women should not do that. And the hardworking Sitabai can't live her life off the jewels.

Sunayana retorted coldly.

Amma was really lucky. She got a dependable maid like Sunguniya. Not everyone is that lucky.

The reply rankled Jaswant Babu. Why does he commit the blunder of mistaking this house for his when he gets told in different ways that he should mind his own business?

What he didn't understand was how could they then think of his house, his belongings, and his savings as theirs and try to stake a claim on them!

Colonel Swamy had reprimanded him on discussing the matter. The truth is that you have gotten into the habit of being unhappy. Every matter feels like an attack.

Actually, this is nothing but the anger old people feel for not being able to get others to obey anymore.

'Now let it go, you've ruled for as long as you could. Till the time you feel like you own the walls of the house, the house can never become a home for the others. Leave it.'

Jaswant Babu thought his advice was sound. Sometimes, his stubborn mind would leave its whim. It'd start ruminating. It had been thinking for a few days. Analysing itself.

Oh! Where is this light shining in his sleep! Jaswant Babu felt that a dream was knocking on his sleep. He was amazed. A dream in his sleep after all these years?

He remembers the wait for dreams. Jaswant Babu could never remember them fully in spite of trying hard to. The sweet incidents would just float around like silk at the edges of his mind. He had been missing dreams since his retirement and was still missing them. The dreams must have thought that they could not deal with the loud snores of the aged.

How did Shivani lose her way today?

The phone in the drawing room rang. Sunayana informed him. He has a call from Trivandrum. She was busy. Which means that Sitabai wasn't done with her work yet. He was very upset. He could not embrace his dream.

A call from Trivandrum meant it was his daughter, Shalini calling.

The slippers under his bed had been moved.

Usually, Shalini called at night. Nobody called after eleven because of the exorbitant STD rates.

Babu Jaswant Singh knew this much. His son-in-law, Mr Chauhan gets telephone reimbursement from his company, ONGC. But he also knew that the limit to it kept changing and whatever spilled over had to be paid out of the salary cheque. Shalini would often try to get Narendra Bhaiyya to call so that she can get to talk to Babuji too. She had told them that her in-laws had ruined them. On the pretext of calls to check on the elder brother-in-law, sometimes father-in-law would start enquiring about lawsuits or start asking about how much sugarcane had been sold by him to government channels? Is Rajnath Singh really trying to improve conditions in Uttar Pradesh or is it only media propaganda?

He was very proud of Shalini. She never said anything to her father-in-law even if she was irritated. She has taken after her mother. Narendra's mother had never argued with her elders nor did she ever appear bare-headed in front of them. Sunayana didn't even have the manners to touch her father-in-law's feet even on festivals.

The call worried him a little.

'Is everything alright? Calling at this hour of the day?'

Sensing worry in his voice, Shalini assured him that there was no reason for anxiety. She was in her husband's office for some work. His boss is in Assam. His phone was free. So she decided to take the opportunity and talk to her father. It had been over fifteen days since they last spoke. How is he doing? Taking medicines on time? Walking every day?

Suddenly Shalini changed track.

'Babuji, why aren't you surrendering the locker in Kanpur?'

The reason for calling in the day, at full rates, wasn't a mystery anymore. The brother and sister have had a discussion. This issue couldn't wait till night.

Narendra had spoken of leaving on Saturday. It is Thursday today.

'Six hundred and fifty rupees is not a small amount in these days of rising inflation. Best to not have pointless expenses.'

Jaswant Babu came to the point.

'Narendra thinks the rent on the locker is pointless. The phone bill is being paid, house tax on the bungalow is being paid, the area's watchman is being paid a salary. Aren't these pointless expenses? As for the jewellery, Shalu, your mother gave you both, whatever she wanted to give, in your weddings.

'I had opened the locker yes, I don't know what is left in it and what is not….'

Shalini drew a long breath. As if in speaking to him, she was breaking a promise.

'There are still a lot of things in the locker, Babuji. A lot of Amma's sets, the five *tola* nose-ring, a lot of silver.

'Amma always said that the Pachladd and Kundan sets were for Anvita and Vikram's wife …'

The argument was pointless.

He doesn't remember if he had ever screamed at Shalini. A reprimand would make her sob for hours. He could never bear her sobs. He'd hold his ears to console her. Please stop crying. He'd never say anything to her. Only then would the waterworks stop.

Jaswant Babu felt himself coming undone. He had never imagined that Shalu would leave his side and argue for her brother and sister-in-law. He had no sympathy left for her. That Shalu who'd ask whether he'd be with them on Sunday and he'd take the next train to Kanpur without a reservation. She hadn't climbed out of his lap when she had got small pox. It had become difficult for him to get up to even shit or piss.

Jaswant Babu's voice raised a bit. She is trying to teach him, why isn't she familiarising her brother and sister-in-law with their responsibilities? They are such clean slates that it is difficult to find two others such as them. He was of the opinion that there was not just one dog but two in the house – Tommy was one and the other was retired civil engineer Jaswant Singh! Tommy was definitely in a better position. His presence gave their house more prestige in the Society. The entire family would fuss over him the entire day. Nobody feels the need to fuss over Jaswant Babu. Tommy is a pedigree dog. Jaswant Babu's presence has besmirched their reputation. Why should they respect him?

His words worried Shalini. She felt that Jaswant Babu's mind was unhinged. He had never spoken with his children in such a way.

She tried to cajole her Babuji. Tried to explain calmly and explain the financial situation too. Babuji was neither trying to live peacefully nor was he letting Bhaiyya and Bhabhi do so. There were misunderstandings cropping up between husband and wife. Bhaiyya was getting caught between his wife and his father. He was so disturbed that he wasn't being able to work properly. It isn't that Bhaiyya doesn't think about Babuji's happiness. That he doesn't face any troubles. He also realises that Amma's sudden death has changed Babuji. Loneliness was eating him up. But in spite of Bhaiyya's attempts the family was not finding peace. Babuji also needs to make an effort. He should not keep obsessing over his dignity in the house. Does she need to explain the importance of family to him? Bhaiyya had thought so far that to keep Babuji engaged and happy, he should keep him there. He has found out about an old age home in Sector 55 of Noida, maybe he should stay there. He'd stay busy in the company of people his age. Bhaiyya has seen the place. He was saying it is beautiful. The food is excellent. If he stays there, Bhaiyya's expenses will shoot up. Bhaiyya is still willing to do that for Babuji's happiness.

Bhaiyya's friend Rajiv Raizada had spoken to him about an ashram in Haridwar. The ashram is on the banks of the Ganga. The evening aarti can be seen from the window even if you don't step out. Bhaiyya is worried about the future too. He could get an appointment letter from the American company in a few months. It was a different matter when Amma was still alive. It won't be prudent to leave him in Kanpur now …

The telephone receiver fell out of Jaswant Babu's hand.

On hearing the receiver crash on the floor, Sunayana rushed towards the telephone. But Jaswant Babu did not look back.

Deep inside him, deeper and yet deeper, the sound of wooden sandals crossing the courtyard, going towards the kitchen echoed and re-echoed. After the first roti is kept aside for the cow, his would be the first thali to be readied and served for he was the patriarch of the house. But, who was this *he*?

Who else but his own father!

# Fourth Absence

भारतीय डाक
INDIA POST

# Flu

Turning sides, Jaswant Babu felt as if his six foot frame had undergone third degree torture. His joints had never pained like this. He couldn't understand how he had gotten a fever without any warning sneezes or coughs. He was not careless about his health – he was proud of his healthy body. There was reason to be proud too. He knew of a lot of friends and acquaintances in Kanpur who had had to get bypass surgeries as soon as they turned fifty. Plasters on legs have become almost routine. Ok, Ok, Jaswant Babu held his throbbing head and reprimanded himself. There was no need to be so arrogant. He should be happy that he was still alive. Not as if Narendra's mother was still around to take care of him.

Doctor Anurag had been stern in telling him to only drink lukewarm water. Sunayana promptly filled a thermos and kept it on the bedside stool. He should take a few sips by himself whenever he feels thirsty. He complained that he could not stand the stale smell of tea, milk or water from a thermos. Sunayana replied calmly. That is only true if the thermos is of low quality. He should be satisfied that his vomiting bouts, after getting Tommy back from his morning ablutions, had worried Sunayana. She woke Narendra up and sent him to Jaswant Babu's room. While taking him to the bed from the bathroom, Narendra realised that the vomiting was not just due of indigestion. He was burning up. The thermometer showed a reading above hundred. It was evident that he had a fever.

Narendra called up Doctor Anurag Chaturvedi requesting him to pay a house visit on his way to the dispensary. Doctor Anurag announced that he had flu and prescribed medicines but added that it was advisable to get cholesterol, urea, sugar, etc., tested immediately. He also informed that a pathologist from S.K. Labs came to Arora Chemists at eight. He must have arrived by now. Narendra should call him home. The report will be at the chemist's by five in the evening. He'll call them up and get the report delivered to his dispensary. He'll change the medicines, if need be. Blood pressure is a little high. He must have been taking medicines for that. He doesn't see the need for increasing the medication...

Jaswant Babu had realised yesterday morning that it would not be possible for him to emerge from the mental agony that Shalini's announcement had caused him. He had lain down for hours without moving a muscle. Wounds after wounds. Colonel Swamy's absence was disturbing him and now this scheme by his own children to send him away! He kept wondering how a father could be forsaken by his own family. What have they done for him? Neither in terms of money, nor has any illness made him dependent on them to rob them of their golden youth! How could Shalu listen to this? Why didn't she protest and argue with brother to take Babuji with him to America? Not that he would have hung from the plane in eagerness. He wasn't even ready to leave Kanpur to move to Delhi.

He agreed to leave only on being coaxed and cajoled. The beloved daughter couldn't even say once that if there's no place at Bhaiyya's, she'll keep Babuji at hers. She'd consider herself lucky to be able to serve him. Babuji never discriminated between the two of them.

Jaswant Babu was on that track again.

Same stories again? Day after day! Every single day! though, he understood that this way he will only harm himself and no one else.

Jaswant Babu got up from the bed suddenly. Thinking, even if for a little while, he could be free of this roof. Aimless walking appealed to him often. Wearing his slippers, he left the house. Sunayana's roar bumped into his back. He was quite familiar with the formality of the roar. He knew that the roar was not to ask politely or with concern why he was leaving home when it was time for the children to be back from school.

Jaswant Babu found himself walking towards Chilla Gaon. There were only three or four cars queueing up at the petrol pump on the right-hand side of the road.

In the next petrol pumb, he found a long queue of autos getting CNG. The stink drew his attention to the garbage dump on the left. He took out the handkerchief from the pocket of his kurta to cover his nose. A herd of cows were looking for food in the garbage.

The freshness of air took away the smell near the board for 'Riverside View'. He was happy to realise that this stench wasn't the kind of stench that had rendered his nostrils incapable of being able to smell anything at all. The handkerchief went back, into the pocket. Jaswant Babu was now moving towards thc newly-built and half-empty Ashiyana right across Shikhar Apartments. Right then the school bus dispersed the waiting crowd on his side of the road. Malay and Nilay might have gone back home. Their bus also probably goes from here. He didn't see it. It is possible that he might have seen it on the way. Ramvati … no, again, the same mistake – Katyayini and Kumudini must also be returning from their schools at this hour. Do they also get off at their gate from their bus?

Jaswant Babu was suddenly saddened. Little Katyayini-Kumudini could probably not even get a rickshaw ride home as from what he remembers, the school is far from home. Sunguniya, Ramratan on her hips, must be rushing to pick them up after finishing the day's work. It is possible that she might have told them that she couldn't leave work and the two should just hold each other's hands and carefully walk back home through the narrow lanes on their own. Such a situation is fraught with danger. Who knows when a car or rickshaw might bump into someone in those narrow lanes!

Jaswant Babu's hand wandered to the pocket of his kurta from under his sweater. He found his wallet in the pocket. He took it out to see how much money he had. Seven notes of hundred gave him the confidence that he was still affluent. He summoned a rickshaw that was crossing by.

He told the rickshaw to take him to Pocket 3. The cold breeze in spite of the sun, made him realise that he had left on a whim and had forgotten to take a muffler or the tamarind-coloured weather-beaten old shawl to cover his shoulders.

He stopped the rickshaw in front of the Post Office in Pocket 3. With the promise that the rickshaw-puller waits there for him to take him back. He wanted to go back home. He will pay him accordingly.

Jaswant Babu will send a money-order of five hundred rupees to Sunguniya at his address in Kanpur. The old postman Hariram knew him. Hope he has not been transferred. Even if Hariram wasn't there, it shouldn't be a problem. Sunguniya knew how to write her name. Narendra's mother had taught her in her free time. He doesn't think she might have forgotten. Even if she has forgotten to, she can get it by giving a thumb print. The only problem was Sunguniya's self-esteem. Jaswant Babu will send a letter with the money order. The money order is not for Sunguniya but for Katyayini and Kumudini's education. He requests that Sunguniya fixes a monthly rickshaw for their commute to and from the school. She shouldn't let them walk. There was a lot of traffic even in the by-lanes. She should get them a tutor if they aren't good at their studies.

She shouldn't even consider returning the money. He will be hurt! Doesn't she want to see her Babuji happy?

Jaswant Babu removed the last lines after writing them! Don't know why. Who knows how the postman is. It was a different matter with Hariram.

He also wrote that he will send five hundred every month. So that there are no obstacles in the way of their education.

Malay opened the door. He asked Dadu angrily where he had gone during lunch-time. Mummy was worried that you didn't even inform before leaving.

There was a plate for him on the dining table. Just one plate. Which meant that the children had eaten. Sunayana asked him if he wanted her to serve him food. Jaswant Babu couldn't tell her that he didn't feel like eating. All he said was that if there was some rice, he could eat a few bites with dal.

He had barely straightened on his bed for a wink after eating that Sunayana closed the door to his room and switched on the TV. The undignified fight in the Lok Sabha over POTA could be heard in his room in spite of the closed door. He could also hear Tommy getting unchained. Tommy was probably interested in the discussion around

POTA. Sunayana was usually careful about him. Cared for him. Suddenly the loud music of MTV starts. She is changing channels for Tommy during ad breaks. Both the children had gone to the neighbour's to study with a friend.

'Babuji, open your mouth, I have to put the thermometer in.' 'Why?' Jaswant Babu got a little unnerved on finding Sunayana standing next to his bed.

'I have to check your temperature.'

Jaswant Babu snapped out of the past. Opened his mouth immediately. Sunayana put the thermometer in his mouth and went out of the room. He had flu. She had to come near him. Doctor Anurag Chaturvedi had directed. He wants to look at the fever chart in the evening.

'How much is it?'

'Quite high, Babuji.'

'Even then,' his eyes were burning up.

'Above hundred and two.'

Sunayana asked him before turning away. What would he like to eat for lunch? Should she make daliya?

He thought to himself. Can a sick person eat sweet daliya? She should make a khichdi with moong dal. His silence was taken as approval by Sunayana, who didn't bother to repeat her query.

Jaswant Babu felt an intense body ache around midnight when he got up to relieve himself. The cold breeze must have gotten to him on the rickshaw ride. He knew it. He'll take a few Disprins with his breakfast.

He'll get fine. He went back to sleep as soon as he lied down.

It became difficult for him to take Tommy out for his ablutions next morning. Jaswant Babu was not even able to get up.

He had asked Doctor Anurag in the evening, impatiently, when will his fever come down? He had decided to take Colonel Swamy's address with him while leaving for his walk the next morning and find his house in Noida's Sector 26.

You will soon be fine, Uncle. It takes about five to six days for the fever to come down. It is better if you don't think about your illness.'

Jaswant Babu will be tied to his bed till then!?

The medicines are working. The headache has become bearable compared to the morning.

He could smell something. Suddenly, his blocked nose has opened up. Was it the smells of the nasal drops? No, someone has left a bouquet of white chrysanthemums near his bedside. Jaswant Babu took long and deep breaths and the fragnance of the flowers was, as if, climbing down the stairs of his consciousness. One-by-one.

'Why is your voice hoarse?' Shivani had called from Aligarh.

'It only wants to hear you today.'

'And what if I told you I called you from this far to hear you?'

'Then, I'd have to say, you should say something from your side as well as something from mine. But you'll have to do all the talking.'

'Stop joking.'

'Tonsils have swollen up.'

'Been to a doctor?'

'Been … have to take Althrocin for the next five days.'

'What's the temperature?'

'Hundred and five … feels like it is going up now!'

'Jokes again! Is somebody around?'

'Yes, someone has just come now.'

'Who?'

'You.'

'Ufff!!'

'Vaidehi would get worried if I informed her in Kanpur. Narendra and Shalini's half-yearly exams are about to start. There's nothing to worry about.'

'You can barely talk,' worry was evident in her voice.

'Ketaki is coming. Cooks whatever random thing she can think of.'

'What time does she come in the morning?'

'Around seven.'

'What time is it right now? Do you have a clock in front of you?'

'It is on the wall – seven fifteen in the evening.'

'I will reach your place in the morning … I'll be up all night too.'

'What'll happen to the students at Aligarh University?'

'They knew you were going to fall sick, which is why they have gone on strike.'

The doorbell of his house in New Shahganj in Agra rang at midnight. He was surprised. Who could it be at this time? His colleagues had visited him in the evening. Neighbours? It had just been three months since he had moved here and their relationship was still formal. It couldn't be the neighbours this late in the night. When Jaswant Babu opened the door, he found Shivani standing in front of him.

Shivani spent the whole night with her palm on his forehead … kept touching his forehead with her lips.

'What will you tell Ketaki in the morning?'

'What should I tell her?'

'The truth.'

'Should I tell Ketaki that she is a friend and I …'

'Tell her that. I'm not scared.'

Why did that boldness get defeated by traditions, Shivani? Why did you become meek and get married wherever your brother told you to? Is it because he couldn't be brave? But, he had never claimed he was...

# Fifth Absence

# Sintex Tank

Jaswant Babu's ears have woken up. He felt as if he hadn't woken up. A part of his body would wake up while he slept and would stay awake the whole night. And make him feel like he wanted to piss. He should wake up or he'll wet the bed. Sometimes, the cough in his throat would tell him to throw it out by coughing or the itchiness would make it difficult for him to sleep. Sometimes his legs would wake up to the fact that they had gone numb – he couldn't even turn sides.

... the phone is ringing. It keeps ringing. Who could it be? Jaswant Babu's ears were getting impatient. It could be a call from Sunayana's home. It could also be Shalu. Though, he had a feeling it may not be Shalu. She couldn't be going to his son-in-law's office every now and then just to call him. Nor would his boss keep taking leaves as per their convenience. What must be the time right now? He should check the alarm clock, kept on the bedside stool. Definitely the time will prove his estimate right. The conversation must have probably started. Not probably, definitely. Sunayana usually never spoke this softly. He had never known her to. He couldn't understand what she was saying over the phone. He couldn't see anything on the clock. He could see fireflies dancing as soon as he opened his burning eyes. He was surprised. He had never been friendly with fireflies. He had captured a few in his hands with his friends as a child but freed them immediately. He has seen them go away from him. Then, how could they be squatting in his eyes?

A few words from Sunayana's softly spoken conversation trickled to him – Sintex tank, theft, backyard, police.

Meaning? Who was on the phone?

Sitabai had been in his room to mop some time ago.

The sound of the moving mopping bucket had struck his eardrums like thunder. He had been sleeping or he wouldn't have shied away from scolding her. Don't clean my room. Can't you see, I am sick. Can't bear the sound.

Sitabai comes around eleven to sweep and mop. Must be twelve. Sunguniya comes at this time to work at Netaji Ram Khilawan's house.

Jaswant Babu had been awake when Sunayana, thinking he was asleep, had informed Narendra who had just returned from work, that Sunguniya had called from Kanpur. She had been eager to speak with Babuji and insisted that his daughter-in-law get him on the phone even if for a minute. She had to discuss something important. On being told that Babuji was sick and could not come to the phone, she said that something important has happened. The small Sintex tank that Babuji had kept in the backyard after replacing it with the big water tank was stolen last night. She went to the police station in the morning to file a report. The police had recieved a call from Netaji. The police assured Netaji that there was nothing to worry about. They'll find the tank in a few days. There's only one problem. It will be difficult to find it if the thief has installed it in his house overnight because all Sintex tanks look alike.

Sunguniya is feeling guilty. She was saying – how will she face Babuji. She is usually a light sleeper. Doesn't know how she couldn't hear anything last night. Sunayana immediately expressed her opinion. She was convinced that the cunning Sunguniya is trying to hide her crime. Who had gone to check whether the tank was there till yesterday?

'That wretch will get the house robbed and will repeat the same story someday … don't know why Babuji doesn't sell the house and free himself of worry.'

Jaswant Babu wanted to scream at Sunayana that she shouldn't … for an ordinary tank … blame Sunguniya … Sun … is his head spinning or is there an earthquake? He wasn't being able to hold his head … where have his hands gone!

# Sixth Absence

HOSPITAL

# Consciousness

When Sunayana came in the morning, after seeing off the children to school, to check on Jaswant Babu, he seemed very conscious to her. She saw him go to the bathroom fully conscious to rinse his mouth and do potty. He asked her as always – what's the temperature? On being told that it was a little above 103, he said the medications have just started. They'll show some result in a few days.

The second question he asked was whether his friend from Noida, Colonel Swamy, had called him yesterday. She said she hadn't received any calls from a man called that but she'll check with Narendra. They had received a lot of calls last night. Narendra would have surely mentioned it if there had been a call for him. Sunguniya had called. He had been sleeping. She didn't want to wake him up. It wasn't that important a matter. She just wanted to ask about him.

He didn't ask any questions after that. His face was set in a way that said that he didn't want to know anything else either. News of the theft of the tank could bother him. The tank got stolen today, tomorrow it could be something else – she thought that and didn't think it right to mention it. She had warned Sunguniya in hushed tones. She was living for free. Is this the kind of watch she is keeping?

He had been fully awake in the morning and looked serene in spite of being in pain. He had called for her as soon as she had turned away after jerking the thermometer and given her five notes of five hundred from under his pillow to foot his medical bill. Keep it. They'll be useful. They are just lying with him anyway. She turned down the offered notes out of habit, not conscious thought. What's with expenses – they get managed. They'll keep managing. But he hadn't agreed.

He had requested for three-four Monaco biscuits before getting his temperature taken. She had kept the biscuits on the tray. He had to be given the medicines after the biscuits. When she had gone to his room to give him the medicines, he had asked her an absurd question while taking water from the thermos.

'Are you the nurse?'

They had never joked with each other. She found his question odd.

'I am Sunayana, Babuji, your daughter-in-law.'

'Daughter-in-law!' His eyes fluttered in disbelief. As if he couldn't see clearly.

'When did you come from Kanpur? Why did you sell the water tank?'

She got worried. Medicines in her fist, she ran to her bedroom. Told Narendra.

Babuji seems delirious. He is saying absurd things. He seems to have lost his mind. He couldn't recognise me. Saying strange things.

'Did you give him the medicines?' On being asked by Narendra she raised her hands skywards. It was beyond her. Here are the medicines. He should give them. She was scared. She will not go to his room ever.

Narendra called up Doctor Anurag Chaturvedi at once.

Doctor Anurag asked him on reaching – 'Uncle, can you tell me your name?'

In a weak voice, he answered, 'My name … you tell me my name. Yes, I remembered … isn't it Harihar?'

'Who is Harihar?' Doctor Anurag asked Narendra.

'He was a close friend of Babuji's.'

'Was?'

'He isn't alive. Died quite sometime ago.'

They walked into the drawing room. Doctor Anurag advised that they shouldn't keep Uncle at home. He should be admitted to the Kailash Hospital in Noida immediately. He is calling for an ambulance. He will go with Narendra. Uncle should stay there for a few days. It will be easier to get all the necessary check-ups done.

He didn't agree to get into the stretcher. Narendra cajoled him. His health had taken a turn for the worse, which is why he was being taken to the hospital for a check-up. He will get him back after the check-up. It isn't too far, just close by, in Noida.

The mention of Noida brightened up his shrivelled face as if he was being taken to his favourite haunt. He got into the stretcher meekly.

# Final Absence

# Body Blow*

The flu was quite a bother. When Jaswant Babu returned to Narendra's house after spending six days at Kailash Hospital, Tommy's jumping-with-joy-feet-licking love made him find his lost patience. He wanted to leave the memory of the hospital stay behind. He was happy that Tommy was helping him in this endeavour.

Last evening, Jaswant Babu mustered courage and went downstairs for a short time in whatever clothes he could manage to wear. The shaken parts of his weak body scared him as soon as he reached downstairs and warned him that his remaining days will be spent dependent on a walking stick. But he should not give up. Stay strong. He could go to the garden adjacent Kirti Apartments and rest in the benches there to make his walks longer and go farther; stiff joints will open up only

---

* The heading of this chapter is *Patkani* which is a term used in kushti, Indian wrestling, where it is a move when a wrestler bodily lifts and flings down his opponent on the floor. Used in the novel to indicate the shock or body blow the protagonist suffers when he discovers the truth.

with effort. The seven days in bed seemed like seven years in *Kaala Pani*.

Jaswant Babu recalled something when he remembered Colonel Swamy's attitude towards death.

Maybe the 'Flu' was the face of death and maybe he could not bear the fierce countenance of death and possibly died. At that moment he felt that there was no harm in having died. There was nothing left to do. But this time, death has made its acquaintance with him. We'll see later which other face it takes on. It is not possible for him to choose it. It might be possible for a few brave souls. They pick up a well, lake, poison, the blade of a fan, the jump from a tall building, river, sea, etc.

He also felt that no matter what justification he gives, death has sensed his inner thoughts and maybe has given him a few more days to live, respecting them. Had he died without meeting Colonel Swamy, he would have always complained about it.

Today's morning is a new beginning for him.

He woke up and decided that today, neither will he waste time in calling on Colonel Swamy's landline, nor will he indulge in negative thoughts while waiting for him on the Mayur Vihar flyover. Last night's walk has invigorated him. He was still physically weak but he won't let this weakness defeat him. He will go straight to the Colonel's house. Not like he was going to walk the distance!

He decided to take an auto to Noida. He will tell the auto driver to wait for a couple of hours. He knew

Colonel Swamy will not let him go without feeding him breakfast. He might not have returned from his trip but his family would also host him. He was no less eager about meeting them. In fact, he is going to take the names of each and every one of them and surprise them by listing out their qualities. He might make a mistake in identifying one or the other of them but in that case, he will ask them their names without any hesitation. Colonel Swamy and he had decided to meet at his place the coming Sunday on many occasions. Inform your daughter-in-law that you will have lunch at a friend's house. That was his offer. It is possible that his daughters-in-law might not let him go back without feeding him dinner. Appu's friends don't come over too often. In that situation, his family will be informed over the phone. He should not worry about the ride back. Shreenarayan will drop him home in the *Jonga*.

Something or the other would come up and their plan would get cancelled.

Suddenly, he'd find out that his middle daughter-in-law, Anushree has to go to Madhya Pradesh to attend the Khajuraho Dance Festival that very day. Her flight is at two-thirty in the afternoon. She had two conditions. The first that Appu takes her to the airport. The second that she wants to meet his beloved friend. If his friend came over while she was away, how will she meet him? It will be better if Appu invites his friend over only after she returns from the Khajuraho Dance Festival. Anushree is the mother of Giligadu. How can he not listen to her? Doesn't matter. They'll make a plan next week. Everyone at home is excited about meeting him.

He told Jaswant Babu about Anushree very excitedly. Anushree is an excellent Bharatnatyam danseuse. She was very thankful for having been invited to the Khajuraho Dance Festival. Her long-cherished desire has been fulfilled. Her guru, S.N. Pillai, had strived that she be invited to the prestigious Khajuraho Dance Festival for a performance. Guru Pillai is annoyed with the politics in the world of Dance in India and maintains that there is no respect for artistes here. Amateurish dancers are winning national awards! It is true that this occasion is no less than a festival for their family.

Giligadu are eagerly waiting for Sunday. They are demanding that they go along to see their mother off at that airport. Katyayini wants to go in the pink frock she had worn for her last birthday. Kumudini wants to wear a black coat on denims. Why do they want to go? They want to see mother get into the plane. Colonel Swamy tried hard to explain to them that they can come along to the airport but they will not be able to see Ma getting into the plane. They tried to defeat him with their lisping replies. Appu is trying to fool them. They have seen in films that people can wave to their relatives getting into planes from the balcony. He cut into their reply. They must have seen that in old films. They should give him the name of any new film. Both the squirrels went quiet. Their innocent faces fell like deflated balloons.

Colonel Swamy could not bear their unhappiness. Had to tell them. They should not be disheartened. He promises. He will send them to their mama's house in Bangalore by flight along with their mother. His beloved Giligadu will fly in the skies like fairies.

'In this matter, Shreenarayan …' Colonel Swamy stopped himself. As if he was shy about something and was in a dilemma about whether he should finish what he was saying or not.

Jaswant Babu did not dig deeper. Colonel Swamy had seemed a little unsettled. Jaswant Babu sensed a deep pain ring out in his voice.

Shreenarayan was not in favour of Anushree going with her guru, Pillaiji, to the Khajuraho Dance Festival. The old man is cranky. What is the need of going with him? The singer, Savitri Amma, will go with her retinue anyway. If Guruji will not go on stage to play the *manjira*, will the *manjira* refuse to clang?

Guruji has had a very interesting past. His first wife had been his disciple. The second wife was the first one's sister; she had also been his disciple. Shreenarayan doesn't like his habit of stoking Anushree's ambitions and taking an interest in them. The result: regular fights between the couple.

Shreenarayan is an introvert. He shies away from expressing his feelings. He feels that there is more to his doubts about Anushree and Guruji's relationship. He wants Anushree to give up on her dance career like her older sister-in-law, Madhavi and devote herself to running the house. That she be focused. Their fights over the Khajuraho Dance Festival continued for a week. Anushree made a decision. She was not going to let go of an opportunity she had waited so long for. Khajuraho Dance Festival is internationally renowned. Only Appu could stop her. If Appu told her to quit dancing, she'd decide that very moment to try and forget her dance. She'll really try.

The situation took a delicate turn. Colonel Swamy realised that he'd have to talk to his son before reaching any conclusion. He'll have to gauge Shreenarayan's feelings and fears. What does he want?

Father and son walked the roads and talked into the night, till one thirty. Shreenarayan made his situation clear. It hurts him that Anushree obeys Guru Pillaiji. To the extent that she does not consult him before taking a decision. Guruji's command is supreme for her. Their house is of no importance to Guruji. He wants all of Anushree's time for dance practice. Katyayini and Kumudini also become secondary to dance. He hadn't told Appu but Guruji had scolded Anushree when she had conceived Katyayini and Kumudini and had forced her to go for an abortion. If becoming a mother is the aim of her life then she should give birth to three or four more kids and stay at home. Take care of the kids. She should forget her dream of becoming the best dancer in the country. She can make babies after reaching that position too. What is the rush? She is not that old. If Anushree had the babies, it was only because of Shreenarayan's warning. He had told her very clearly: The day she goes for an abortion, she'd find his corpse hanging in the room.

He advised his son. It is important to understand yourself before understanding your wife. You can understand someone else only after having understood yourself. It is Anushree's discipline that forces her to heed her guru's commands. As for Katyayini and Kumudini, it is his envy that's making him find fault in a mother's devotion to her children. He has never felt it. The girls are her life. There are a lot of people in the house to look after them. That's what families are for. It is the strength of a family that helps you tide over difficult situations. He is of the opinion that though Katyayini and Kumudini are young they should realise that their mother is not an ordinary woman. She is a famous artiste. As for balance, he feels there is no need for a discussion on it, just adjustments on both sides. Balance can't come from one side alone.

The whole family had to be called for a discussion. He made Katyayini and Kumudini attend too.

He said only one thing to Anushree – that she closes her eyes and focuses on her inner self. Look within. What does her heart tell her? The heart always speaks the truth. Without any doubts. Without any biases.

All eyes were on Anushree.

Five minutes went by. He told her to open her eyes.

Suddenly Anushree started bawling. Everybody was shocked.

'I can't live without dance, Appu!'

Shreenarayan opened his mouth to protest. Colonel Swamy raised a finger gesturing him to be silent.

'Anushree has mustered the strength to speak the truth, something Madhavi could never do. We have to respect the truth.'

Shreenarayan touched his feet in the morning before he left for his walk. Anushree was standing behind him. She also touched his feet, 'Appu! We need your blessings.'

Shreenarayan gave him the good news. There will be a puja in the house on Sunday morning after his walk. To pray for Anushree's success.

Jaswant Babu confronted Colonel Swamy. He often discussed Madhavi but never spoke much of Anushree. Why?

Colonel Swamy said just this, 'How could I, friend! Not just for my son, but she had always been Giligadu's mother for his father too!'

❖

Suddenly the curtain on the right side of the auto fluttered in the wind and stroked Jaswant Babu's face. He couldn't find the string to tie the curtain. On being asked the auto driver told him the string wasn't there.

He had to move towards the right hand side and tuck the curtain down under his foot. Jaswant Babu also felt that was the right thing to do. The wind wasn't that chilly but he could still feel it. He had thought, he has just gotten better, should wear a monkey cap. But he had found his thought funny. He was going to Colonel Swamy's house for the first time. The daughters-in-law might laugh at him. They shouldn't think he is the watchman.

'It isn't possible for me to stay at home fearing the cold. Morning walks are heavenly. There is a quarter of brandy in the pocket of my shorts. I'd take a swig as soon as I feel even a little cold.'

A smile played on Jaswant Babu's lips. Colonel Swamy has an amazingly colourful personality. In fact, colourful is an inadequate word for his lifestyle. He didn't know how to play with words. He could never think of the right words. Not even when he was with Shivani. He'd feel like uprooting his words as soon as they got even a little poetic.

He requested the auto driver to stop at a sweet shop for a minute as soon as they crossed Nagarjuna Society.

It is not appropriate to go empty-handed to a family. He should get some diamond-shaped Kaju barfis for Giligadu. Colonel Swamy had told him about their favourite sweets. They didn't ask for Kaju barfis – but always asked for diamond shaped barfis. What else do they like? He tried to remember. He is their grandfather number two. Colonel Swamy had painted a terrifying picture of him in front of them – like a giraffe. Giligadu would try to reach him, fluttering their button-like eyes.

He remembered as soon as he crossed the Nirula's after the roundabout. Giligadu liked the chocolate cake and ice-cream from Nirula's. The night they had gone to the bar in Nirula's, Colonel Swamy had especially gotten the chocolate cake packed for them when they were leaving. He thought that he should also get ice-cream and chocolate cake packed for them. If there was a sweet shop ahead, he'd pick up some barfis too.

Won't the ice-cream melt while looking for Colonel Swamy's house?

It is quite cold. His doubt would have been valid had it been summer.

The cake was quite big – almost two kilos. The children are always an excuse but the whole family eats it.

Had Colonel Swamy been with him, he'd have certainly dragged him into the bar for a session.

Jaswant Babu couldn't find a sweet shop in spite of keeping a sharp eye on the roadside. He was disgruntled.

'Which Sector do you want to go to, Bauji?' The auto-driver enquired without turning around.

'Twenty-six.' He had told the driver before getting into the auto.

'Sector twenty-six is on this side of the road, Bauji. Which block?'

'E'. The flats with balconies perched on rounded pillars attracted his attention. He was greeted by greenery as soon as he entered the gates. His heart was filled with joy.

He couldn't hide his impatience.

'Stop the auto and ask someone where E block is. We'd waste time just roaming around.'

A lady was coming in their direction. She seemed annoyed at being stopped by the auto-driver. This is 'G' block. You have come in the opposite direction. You should have taken the first right after entering the gate. E block is at the end of that lane.

E block has started.

Jaswant Babu told the auto-driver Colonel Swamy's house number – we have to go to 303.

They didn't have to take too many narrow lanes.

'There's 303.' The driver said triumphantly, revved up the accelerator a few times and then cut off the engine.

Jaswant Babu's sad face lit up. He asked the driver.

'Help me get down.'

The driver jumped out and took the ice cream and cake boxes from him. Then helped him get off with his other hand. Before taking the stairs, Jaswant Babu tried to get a sense of which floor Colonel Swamy's house is on by looking up.

'It is on the third floor, Bauji, should I drop the things upstairs?'

Jaswant Babu analysed his strength in reply. Realised that in spite of his excitement, his weak body was refusing to walk up three floors. There was no other option, it had to walk up. The cake box would definitely bother. On top of that, it has to be carried carefully, so that the icing doesn't smudge. He has gotten the names of the twins written on it. He wanted that as soon as Giligadu open the box, they should laugh aloud on seeing their names on it. Jaswant Babu also wanted to pamper them like their Appu.

He hadn't taken anything for Colonel Swamy. Should he have taken flowers? Or his favourite whiskey – *Royal Challenge*, although he has no dearth of alcohol. His quota from the Army Canteen wasn't just enough for him but for his friends too. He hadn't thought of it before. No point regretting now.

The driver is behind him. His excitement about meeting Colonel Swamy has probably given a stranger's legs strength too. He felt he was scared for no reason. He was very weak but not so much that he couldn't have climbed up the stairs. He had thought of something downstairs. That he call out to Colonel Swamy and get him to come downstairs. The next moment he had to pity his stupidity. Has Retired Civil Engineer Jaswant Singh gone senile? These are housing societies. He will die of shame if someone else peeked out and commented on his behaviour.

The stairs are quite broad and comfortable.

Colonel Swamy had thought it strange that his room is in the balcony. His suggestion was that if the flat is small, tell your son to buy a house in Noida. He'd get a much bigger house in Noida in that budget. Work on a new flyover has begun. Pay the toll tax and reach South Delhi in a few minutes. All the best restaurants. Parks, clubs, golf course, what not, sit wherever you want, eat whatever you want, have fun. The way he lives. The old trees that he feels Mayur Vihar, Phase 1 lacks are flourishing in Noida. Jaswant Babu knew it was pointless talking to Narendra about this issue. No cure for capital fever. The house in Kanpur was four times bigger. He could have moved there taking cognizance of his father's old age. Talent would have found employment there as well. But only if he had the desire. Desire and a sense of responsibility.

'Oh!' He had noticed the trees with thick trunks. On the branches of which parrots were always playing the whole day long, that tree is right across Colonel Swamy's house, he had said. He'll meet the trees with him on his way back. He'll see the parrots too. He'll see them from his balcony, if possible...

His laboured pants forced Jaswant Babu to take the support of the railing.

Flipped his wrist to check the time. Would Giligadu have returned from school? It is eleven fifteen. Colonel Swamy had told him the time of their return but he couldn't remember it in spite of trying hard to. Again that shimmer! Pulls and drops him in a maze.

Jaswant Babu wanted Giligadu to be behind Colonel Swamy, jumping and screaming, when the door opened. He'll quickly offer them the cake box and ask if they have recognised him. He is their grandfather number two. He got the chocolate cake from Nirula's for them. And Cassata ice-cream, tasty-tasty.

Taking the boxes from the driver, Jaswant Babu thanked him and decided that he is not going to ring the bell of 303 till his breath had settled. There seemed to be only two flats on the floor. 302 had the nameplate of one Mr M.N. Shrivastava and 303 that of his great friend, Colonel Swamy.

He got impatient and rang the bell. How do the breaths matter! He could understand that he was eager to meet Colonel Swamy. The thirteen days seemed like thirteen years. There was no sound from near the door. Rang the bell again. The third was a longer bell. Checked the latch. The latch couldn't inform him whether the residents were at home or not. His excitement had ebbed. He was left wondering. Where had he gone with the family? He had the same complaint again. He could have informed him over the phone if he had to go. This was the first time he was angry at Colonel Swamy's strange behaviour. Should he go down or check with the neighbours. It is possible that the family had gone somewhere outside Noida. The neighbours would at least inform them that he had paid a visit and wanted to check on them. How much he is missing him!

What if the neighbour was like Jaswant Babu's balcony neighbour?

Shyness tried to stop him. Jaswant Babu didn't let the attempt succeed. The neighbours could be good people. Not like he was going to their house to eat!

He went ahead and rang M.N. Shrivastava's bell.

He heard footsteps. The door opened. A soft-looking woman with salt and pepper hair, who could be called beautiful, looked at him questioningly.

'Yes?'

Jaswant Babu hesitated.

'I am a friend of Colonel Swamy's. I have come to meet him.'

'Where have you come from?'

'From nearby, Mayur Vihar. Actually, he hasn't come for walks in a while. So, I thought I'll go to his house and meet him … is nobody at home?'

The lady's voice sounded irritated.

'He is your friend and you don't know?'

'Ma'am?'

'Your friend, Colonel Swamy is no more.'

'Meaning?'

'He is dead. Passed away.'

Jaswant Babu couldn't understand whether his head was spinning or the building was shaking. Or just the doorstep where he stood. His hand shot up to steady himself against the wall of 302.

The lady was alerted by his misstep. She took his hand, supporting him and invited him in.

He sat in the sofa in the drawing room and the lady went in to get a glass of water for him. She took the boxes from his hand kept them on the side.

The water was cold. He gestured to her to warm it a little.

Not only did she warm the water but put two spoons of glucose in it. He drank the water and sat there still, resting against the backrest. I'll make you some coffee. You'll feel better.'

Jaswant Babu couldn't refuse her offer though he wanted to.

The lady turned around in worry on her way to the kitchen.

'Are you fine? You don't need a doctor?'

'I am fine … my account is yet to be settled Mrs Shrivastava.' Hope he hadn't made a mistake in addressing the lady?

Jaswant Babu suddenly realised that his strange statement would not have given the lady any confidence. He wasn't in the frame of mind to instil confidence. But even then, he realised that making a stranger worry for him was an abuse of her hospitality.

He clarified, 'I am trying to gather the strength to deal with the situation.'

Mrs Shrivastava made a cup of coffee for herself too. Must have thought that by giving him company in drinking the coffee, she'd free Jaswant Babu of inhibitions so that he could gather his strength, something he needed.

'When…'

'It has been twelve days since his death. It was the morning of thirtieth November.

'He had left for his morning walk as usual. He must have gone down seven or eight steps when he felt a tremendous pain in his chest. He was incapacitated by the pain and sat on the stairs. After a while, he gathered courage and rang our doorbell. Mr Shrivastava opened the door. On finding him soaked in sweat, he sat him down on the sofa and called the family doctor. On seeing him, the doctor immediately told us that he had suffered a heart attack. No point wasting time in making the rounds of the nursing home. He should be rushed to Emergency in Apollo. He suffered another heart attack on the way to Apollo which he could not bear.'

Where was Jaswant Babu at the time?

Waiting for him on the same flyover in Mayur Vihar. His eyes filled up. Death also came like this. On the stairs. The same stairs he had crossed.

'Where were the children?'

'Which children?' Mrs Shrivastava's question surprised Jaswant Babu.

'Madhavi, Anushree, Giligadu ... his son Shreenarayan.'

'We have seen him alone for the last eight years.'

Jaswant Babu felt like someone had flung him down from the second floor.

Shocked, he kept looking at Mrs Shrivastava open and close her lips. What is Madam saying! Was he imagining things?

Mrs Shrivastava was speaking, a thick fog seemed to be spreading around.

The fog was engulfing Jaswant Babu.

It was 1994. Colonel Swamy was left alone after his wife's death. All three sons had moved to different cities to further their career. Kept making false promises that they will get their father to live with them as soon as possible. After a while, they had built small flats in Bangalore and Hyderabad. Shreenarayan had paid him a visit last summer. From Hyderabad.

He had a special agenda. That Appu was keeping a four bedroom flat in Noida for no reason. He should sell the flat and divide the money among the three brothers. Their small flats had started bothering them. All three had bought land in their cities and now wanted to make bungalows and live in airy houses as soon as possible. They needed a lot of money to make their dream homes. They didn't want to get into the hassle of taking loans. And why should they when they had a solution at home!

Colonel Swamy had sold an expensive plot of land in Ghaziabad to help them in buying the flats. He rejected Shreenarayan's proposal. An angry Shreenarayan had hit his father. Colonel Swamy's screams had worried Mrs and Mr Shrivastava. They knocked on his door. Shreenarayan told him to not open the door and told them to not involve themselves in their domestic dispute. A worried Mr Shrivastava dialled 100 and called the police for help. The police got the door opened. A blood-soaked Colonel Swamy was rushed to Kailash Hospital. As soon as he could speak, he refused to file an FIR against his son. Shreenarayan had caught hold of his feet and was apologising, pleading.

Jaswant Babu had mentioned Anushree. He should hear about her too. No less of a tragedy. She abandoned her year-and-a-half old twins to move in with her dance master. The grandchildren had been raised by their grandmother. They had been admitted to Apeejay School right here. Shreenarayan took them away when their grandmother died. Shreenarayan remarried in spite of Colonel Swamy's opposition and got the girls admitted in a hostel in Hyderabad. Colonel Swamy had put pictures of the girls all over the house. The girls used to call him up without their father's knowledge whenever they could. He'd often visit the girls in Hyderabad without telling Shreenarayan. Stayed at the hostel. Wouldn't let any relative know, he had told them. The hostel warden was the widow of a close friend of his in the Army.

'It is better to not have any children than such butcher children. We are not unhappy that we have no children ...' Mrs Shrivastava started choking up.

They had put him in the mortuary.

Informed the eldest son and his wife in Bangalore.

It was with great difficulty that they managed to find the number of artiste Madhavi of the Academy in Bangalore. Mrs Shrivastava had remembered that she had been awarded the Academy Award last year. They hadn't been able to find contact details at home in spite of repeated searches. The husband and wife reached

Delhi in the evening by flight. They told them that the other two brothers will not be able to attend the funeral. It is difficult to reach on time by train. Flight tickets are not possible for them. Colonel Swamy was cremated on the first. They didn't have the time to wait for the *Chautha*. They returned to Bangalore after collecting the ashes and bones. Said that elaborate funeral rites and rituals were prescribed in their culture. Must be so. Since their relatives were there, they would perform the rites there, they said.

Mrs Shrivastava didn't know if they took anything from the house. Didn't feel the need to either. The eldest son had made a request to Shrivastavaji. He had helped a lot. Could he please do one more favour? They wanted to sell the house. Please inform the property dealers in the area. 303 is on sale. Please give them the phone number in Bangalore. They'll come as soon as there's any news. They'll get the death certificate and wrap up all the bank work at that time. They wanted to sell his things too. It was of no use to them. In fact, they are surprised that Appu still had a black and white television.

Children from the slums would visit Colonel Swamy at around four in the evening for tuitions. He used to spend almost half of his income on these children. He was independent. He used to make such soft idlis. He used to feed the children medu vada and idlis very lovingly. The children were saddened to hear of their teacher's death when they came to study, as always. They wept over his dead body the next day. They weren't letting the body go for cremation. Their parents got them under control with great difficulty.

Mrs Shrivastava couldn't control herself. Wiped a tear with the corner of her sari.

Jaswant Babu got up to hide his own tears, turned his face away and with folded hands said, 'I'll take your leave.'

'The *Terahvin* ceremony must be getting done in Bangalore today. Pray for him. If there is a God, he should give his soul some peace.'

'Wait.' Mrs Shrivastava offered him his cake and sweet boxes the next moment. 'Your boxes.'

'Do the kids from the slums not come any more?'

'Who'd they visit? Their teacher isn't alive.'

'Can you go to the slums?'

Mrs Shrivastava was quiet for a while.

'I can.'

'If you can, can you please distribute the cake and ice cream among the children … why should they be deprived of the prasad of *Terahvin*?'

Mrs Shrivastava kept waiting at the stairs till he was within sight.

Jaswant Babu sobbed on taking each step while coming down with the support of the railing. Which stair was it? He didn't want to step on that stair. He wanted to touch and feel it. Doesn't matter where he lost his life, his breaths had started stopping from here.

# Breaking with Tradition*

Jaswant Babu went looking for the trees with thick trunks as soon as he reached the ground floor. The trees weren't too far. How could he not meet them, those trees on which a thousand parrots of different kinds, were perched, whose calls and variety took him back to Kanpur and reminded him of the old banyan tree opposite his house there.

How many times Colonel Swamy had saved these parrots from hunters. He had handed over a few to the police too. He had given strict instructions to the watchmen in Sector 26 that they not let any suspicious man into the colony who carried a big bag.

Jaswant Babu didn't touch the ancient Neem tree but rested his head on its trunk, tried feeling it with his eyes closed. He felt like he had been touched by a divine

---

* The heading of this chapter is *Atma-tarpan* which literally means performing one's own funeral rites (and other rituals for the departed soul) by oneself prior to death, usually done when you have no children or successors. In the novel it has been used to indicate the protagonist's decision to break away from tradition and rewrite societal rules.

force. He had never seen Colonel Swamy resting his head on the trunk but felt that he too must have also felt the same divine power had he done so.

Maybe the soul of the Neem is his soul too.

Maybe his soul rests in the trunks of all the ancient trees in the locality. He rested his head on the right side of the auto, tucked the flying curtain under his knee and saw the fast running road through the windscreen.

He felt strange. And why did he feel like he was seeing two of everything when he opened his eyes!

He had gotten his cataract operated upon ages ago and his lenses had been working fine till now. His power had increased a little last year but had been working fine. He had never had this complaint before, had he?

The driver looked at him carefully in the rear-view mirror on the side. He had seen him before too and kept glancing on and off.

'Bauji is everything fine … why don't you dry your tears?'

'A man can only live for as long as he is destined to, Bauji.'

The mystery behind his tears was now out that something bad had happened and he was not being able to find peace.

Jaswant Babu was taken aback at his words. His hands wandered to his eyes.

The double vision was bothering him. The driver wasn't wrong.

He could not remember when he had shed so many tears.

He searched his pockets to look for a handkerchief. Why was the handkerchief crumbling like paper in his hands?

He was only getting crumpled hankies after the wash. He was used to starched and pressed handkerchiefs. He had asked Sunayana, there's no need for starch now. She should get his hankies ironed as it is. Sunayana had replied that ironing is very expensive in Delhi. The washerman will charge two rupees for that scrap of cloth. Numbers matter here, not the size.

Jaswant Babu was saddened to feel the paper with the hanky. He tried to find out what kind of a paper was in his pocket after wiping his eyes with the hanky. He remembered that he had put Colonel Swamy's phone number on a piece of paper and kept that in his coat pocket. Written in the Colonel's handwriting. Yes, there was another piece of paper which had Colonel Swamy's address.

Jaswant Babu was amazed to find that it wasn't any other piece of paper but the long lost poem by Anima Das. How hard he had searched for Anima Das's long poem. The poem had also played hide and seek with him. Neither Colonel Swamy nor he could remember its whereabouts. All he had said that if he ever crossed paths with Anima Das's poem, he should read it.

His eyes were welling up again. He touched the paper against his head and promised his friend with trembling lips – I found the poem, friend! He'll never lose it now that he has found it. He'll keep it carefully. He'll read it closely. Each and every line. He'll tell him. He had wanted to know – How is Anima Das's long poem? What did he think of it?

When will Jaswant Babu read it? At night? Night was too far away. He didn't want to waste time. He got impatient. Why not now? He had bifocal glasses. He could read. He should read it.

He wiped his eyes with his handkerchief and started reading Anima Das's long poem.

❖

Babu Jaswant Singh, son of Thakur Samarendra Bahadur Singh, village Sagwar, Post Sagwar, Unnao district (U.P.) is changing his will. He didn't want to follow family traditions. He wanted to write new rules in the annals. He doesn't understand why people do not take the risk of changing their wills. Why don't they understand that it isn't possible to live your life without changing your will?

Now, Jaswant Babu does not want his life to pause. He has just decided that before taking the auto to Glaxo Apartments, he'll take it first to the market. He will get 'Goyal Travel Agent' to book a ticket in Shatabdi to Kanpur for the day after tomorrow. Then, he'll reach home and call up Netaji Ram Khilawan Yadav and ask him to put Sunguniya through. It was one in the afternoon and Sunguniya must be wrapping up her work.

Jaswant Babu wanted to tell Sunguniya: He is fine with whatever she wants to call their relationship. She needs to make the choice, he won't. He knows that she can choose a name and even give it one. Truth be told, he had been living the relationship subconsciously. He would have continued living it thus, had he not chanced upon Anima Das's long poem.

Jaswant Babu will tell Sunguniya to just listen to him today. Just him. He won't be able to say what he wants to say ever again. He wants to live this part of his life with his Giligadu – Katyayini and Kumudini. He wants to incorporate the banyan tree opposite the house in Kanpur into the house. He can't forget that a bird calls out before he wakes up and then goes on to wake up other birds as if playing kho-kho. The second wakes up the third, the third the fourth till there is a chorus of birds singing a symphony which fills his soul with happiness …

Jaswant Babu also wanted to tell Sunguniya that he'll talk to his lawyer, Munna Singh Kushwaha, as soon as he reaches Kanpur. He'll get a new will drawn up and get it registered saying that the house in Kanpur is not ancestral property. He had built it with his own money. After his death, Sunguniya will be the sole owner of the house. He wants to rent a new locker in the bank in her name. So that there is no dispute in the future. Even if there are challenges, Sunguniya will be able to tackle them.

He knows what Narendra's reaction will be. He will certainly be hurt by Jaswant Babu's unprecedented behaviour. He will hate him. It is possible that he won't even come for his cremation when Jaswant Babu dies. Jaswant Babu doesn't want to drag him into pointless people-pleasing. He will be solely responsible for whatever is happening and whatever will happen. He will tell Sunguniya and put it down in his will that he be cremated by Sunguniya's son, Ramratan nee Abhishek Aasre. He, Jaswant Babu, is giving him that right.

Sunguniya should keep lunch ready for him. He'll only have breakfast in Shatabdi. She knows what he likes.

He wanted to say a lot of things to Sunguniya. But he'll stop himself thinking they'll have time for a lot of conversation now. It is not good to be so eager. Only this much and till here on the phone.

# Glossary

| | |
|---|---|
| Aalaap/Alap | The melodic improvisation of a raga, forming a prologue to the formal expression |
| Appu | Father in Malayalam |
| Arnica | Homeopathic medicine to treat pain, insect bites, chapped lips, arthritis and acne |
| Bauji | Father. Also respectful address for an elder |
| Bhabhi | Brother's wife |
| Bhaiyya | Brother |
| Chautha | Fourth day after a death. Part of the funeral rites and mourning period extending to 13 days after death. |
| Gaz | A measurement for land. I sq. gaz=0.990399 sq.metres |
| Gili-danda | A game played with a short stump and a stick. The stump is hit with the stick and made to 'fly'. The farther it lands the higher the score |
| Guddi | Affectionate form of address, a term of endearment for a girl child often continued when she is grown up too |
| Kayamchuran | An Ayurvedic purgative |
| Kaala Pani | A jail sentence or exile to the Cellular Jail, Port Blair, Andaman & Nicobar Islands during British rule was referred to as kaala paani (Black waters). Considered the severest punishment for sedition or treachery against the Crown. |
| Manjira | A cymbal like musical instrument used in Carnatic Music where it is called *Nattuvangam.* |

| | |
|---|---|
| Mawa | Also known as khoya, an ingredient for making sweets made by boiling and solidifying milk |
| Mundan | A ritual shaving of head. Usually after death in the family in the case of adults. And on completion of one year for children |
| Munger | A deep fried snack made from ground pulses. |
| Neta | Leader, Minister |
| Patkani | This is a term used in kushti, Indian wrestling, where it is a move when a wrestler bodily lifts and flings down his opponent on the floor. Used in the novel as chapter heading to indicate the shock or body blow the protagonist suffers when he discovers the truth. |
| Rasaje | An Indian syrupy delicacy common to Uttar Pradesh |
| Supari | Betel nut |
| Talukdar | Tax collector |
| Tauji | Father's elder brother. Respectful form of address for any elder in north India |
| Terahvin | Thirteenth day after a death. Part of the funeral rites, it is the closing ceremony and official declaration that the period of mourning is over and the departed soul proceeds on its journey to the other world |
| Tola | A measure for gold. 1 Tola=1.66 grams |
| Triphala | An Ayurvedic medicine to aid digestion. It is not as strong as *Kayamchuran* but taken with warm water, it can induce smooth bowel movement |